THE
Butterfly
CIRCUS

To my sister Selina, for making that
first special place for me to write.

First published 2019 by Walker Books Ltd
87 Vauxhall Walk, London SE11 5HJ

2 4 6 8 10 9 7 5 3 1

Text © 2019 Francesca Armour-Chelu
Map and postcard illustration © 2019 Francesca Armour-Chelu
Cover design © 2019 Walker Books Ltd

This book has been typeset in Palantino

Printed and bound by CPI Group (UK) Ltd, Croydon CR0 4YY

British Library Cataloguing in Publication Data: a catalogue
record for this book is available from the British Library

ISBN 978-1-4063-8436-9

www.walker.co.uk

THE Butterfly CIRCUS

FRANCESCA ARMOUR-CHELU

WALKER
BOOKS

Contents

1

Chrysalis to Butterfly

I reach the top first. Belle's getting slower. To see her limbs, like a daddy-long-legs, you'd think she'd find climbing easy, but in this game being short has its advantages; I always beat her to the top.

It's bat-black up here and there's nothing to see. I don't need my glasses for getting up the *corde lisse* – I could do that in my sleep. But I put them on now, tie them tight and glance down. Thirty feet below, the circus ring gleams silver. The sawdust is mixed with mother of pearl shavings to make it glow in the dark; that way Belle and I can just about see when the lights go down. Mrs Fratellini doesn't want the audience to spot us climbing. She's the ring mistress. What she says goes.

"It's all about de illusion! Tansy! Belle! You are de actual butterflies of de Butterfly Circus," she often coos. "Butterflies don't climb like de crawly-creepies. You arrive in de darkness. De lights go up! De audience dee-scoover you high above dem! As eef by magic! You are be-ootiful, gleettering!" She clasps her powdered face with her bejewelled hands and gets a little teary at the wonder of it all. "If only my darrrling Alfredo could see you now. How proud he'd be!"

We are the last act; Silks and Flying Trapeze. Our silks are dyed deepest emerald to palest lime and drape to the ground below. They are leaves for us to be caterpillars on. Then we'll be chrysalises before evolving into butterflies. Our act is what everyone really wants to see. Not just because we're the best thing Mrs Fratellini has ever seen, or the best thing *anyone* has ever seen on the Isle of Gala, but because of the safety net. Or lack of one. There's applause when we land, but the near misses get the biggest gasps.

"A net?" Mrs Fratellini once asked, her beady eyes squinting as she thought about it. "Nets are for catching de butterflies. My two butterflies flutter free!"

"Free to break our necks you mean," Belle had muttered. She was only seven then and we hadn't been at the circus long. It's hard to believe there was a time when Belle didn't realise how lucky we are that the Fratellinis found us and put a canvas over our heads. Now, she never stops telling me how we must be "the best of the best" to earn our place here, or else risk ending up in Scoria. And in case we forget, every Found Day when Belle and I blow out our candles as the troupe finish singing, Mrs Fratellini wipes away a tear saying, "To fink, if my dear Alfredo hadn't found you, you could have been got by de wolves!"

She doesn't mean real wolves, although plenty of those roam the old forests of Gala, where we were found. She means the showmen who run the freak shows, where you can pay a single florin to see a pig with two heads, a swan with red feathers or a man covered with fur. Even if you're not a freak, the showmen have ways of turning you into one. But the Butterfly Circus isn't like those stick-and-rag shows. It might not be the biggest, but of all the circuses on Gala it's the most famous; maybe the most famous show on any of the Pleasure Isles, the five biggest islands of the archipelago. That's why the Mainlanders flock here.

The clowns are about to come on. The darkness around the ring twinkles with the Glowbells we sell; glass balls no bigger than a walnut, filled with phosphorescent beads that splash coloured light when you shake them. I tighten my wrist wraps and check that I've got enough rosin on my palms to help me grip. It's made from pine sap and smells like a forest at midnight. It reminds me of something, but the memory scampers away before I can catch it.

Suddenly, the circus ring is bathed in light. Children screech as Boris and Doris tumble in, wearing red enamel wings with black dots. They are the carpet clowns who keep the audience bent double with laughter in order to stop them looking up; that way Belle and I can check the ropes unobserved. Their act is simple. Naughty Doris torments Boris, who's stupid. I've seen them a million times so I know what's happening without watching. Doris sets fire to Boris and a plume of black smoke shoots out of Boris's bottom. I lean out to look. Sure as eggs is eggs, Doris is wafting a huge peacock feather fan by Boris's bottom and the children in the audience are laughing hysterically. Soon, Boris will run in circles, trying to outrun the fire, then Doris will chuck a pail of water over Boris. It'll go wrong and Doris will get the soaking.

There's a gentle thud on the opposite pedestal. Belle's there. I can just about make out her silhouette against the blackness of the tent's cupola. Even though my eyes are not the best, I have a knack for sensing her.

I worry when I hear her wheezing; the climb's tough for her. I imagine her breath as a sooty little moth fluttering across the dark to find me. She rubs some more rosin between her hands, then whistles two low notes to let me know she's ready. The orchestra strikes up as Boris and Doris somersault out. The spotlight cuts and we're plunged into darkness again. We're on. Any second now.

My heart's somersaulting too and my muscles twitch. I'm so excited even my butterflies have butterflies. Here comes the drum roll. The two spotlights go up, hovering between us in the space we call the Hemisphere. Tiny specks of dust swirl in the beams, like a miniature Milky Way. It's so beautiful that I still catch my breath even though I've seen it a thousand times. Then the lights sweep left to find me, making the pink sequins on my costume sparkle.

The second the spotlights land on me I grow many shadows, and together we take a low bow to the deafening applause. But by the time we lift our heads again, the spotlights have flounced off to find Belle, leaving me shadow-less and alone in the dark. Under its cover I quickly pull the silks downwards, testing their tension, getting a sense of them, their feel, as though they're a living creature. In the meantime, the spotlights find Belle. Her costume is embroidered with sapphire sequins, and silver stars twinkle in her curly black hair, twisted in the same way as mine into two pointy coils to look like antennae. Belle says I'm her little candle because I'm so white and my hair's the colour of flame. Really my hair's orange, not bright like a robin's breast – more stale egg yolk actually – but "flame" sounds nicer.

During practice Belle says, "Trust me and jump!" but in performance, we have a secret code: she always blows me a kiss before we start. It's barely airborne before she snatches it back with a wink. It's our ritual, our good luck charm; the very last thing we do before we fly. She'll give me that kiss for real when we're back in the dressing room, picking glitter out of our hair.

Except when I collect my kiss tonight I will have *really* earned it; because I've got a surprise for her, for everyone. Something very special.

It's time. Belle reaches up for the silks and I do the same, my eyebrows scrunched with concentration. Timing is everything. We mirror each other, as if we're the other's shadow. Belle pulls herself up and her biceps ripple. She makes a foot-lock, hooking her leg around the fabric and then, with her other foot, wraps the cloth over to make a stirrup.

Synchronised, we slink upwards, then, when we can climb no higher, we pinch the silks between our legs and let our bodies drop forwards. Weaving one arm through the silks, we brace our backs against the cloth and do the splits, extending our arms. For a moment we are suspended, as if frozen mid-leap, the silks fanning out from our feet. The crowd gasp.

We start to twirl, gently at first, like sycamore seeds and then we slide down, our silks fluttering. As we whirl faster, the silks wrap around us until we're completely cocooned. We wait for a few seconds, then we tumble out and tug two ribbons at the back of our costumes. In a haze of violet gauze, we sprout butterfly wings speckled with chips of turquoise abalone shell. We dangle for a moment as applause floods the tent. Now that we're butterflies, we grab our trapeze bars for our first trick: a double layout.

Belle hooks her legs over the bar and drops backwards, her strong arms sweeping in deep, graceful arcs. She is my catcher. I'm the flyer; the real star of the show. I grip the bar and drop backwards too, curling my knees close to my chest and then under the bar. I cast out, swinging my feet up into the highest point of the Hemisphere. When the trapeze completes its return sweep, I beat back a second, then throw my legs up in front of me as hard as I can. I repeat the swing and beat back once more, before letting my legs fly forwards. Their momentum is so strong I'm pulled after them until I'm upside down. It's perfect.

Trust me and jump!

I let go of my bar and fly. It's what I do night after night, but each time it's the most beautiful, most terrifying thing. I'm flying fifty feet in the air, spinning in a blaze of colour with nothing but make-believe wings of net and sparkling shell. I complete two perfect somersaults, then I swoop down towards Belle, who is rising up to meet me. She plucks me from my flight and delivers me safely to the board. I land in a cloud of chalk, like I've jumped in fresh snow.

That's what's meant to happen.

But this time, as I start to fly, I begin a *triple* somersault. I know I can do it; I know I can earn that kiss, that rapturous applause. I have the height and speed to get one more turn before she catches me. Timing is everything. But as I start the third turn, I see Belle's trapeze is already swinging away. I still reach for her outstretched hands, even though I know she can't possibly catch me. Belle screams my name as I scream hers and our fingertips brush. I'm still spinning and dropping with sickening speed. Faster and faster, so fast even the spotlights can't keep up. I'm lost in the dark; alone and falling.

A few seconds before I hit the ground, something cold and soft swipes against my palm. I grab it and my arm is wrenched back with a snap, but nothing can stop my descent. My last thought is *I'm going to...*

2

Butterfly to Bug

But I didn't.

When I opened my eyes, three days later, the first person I saw was Belle, crumpled as an autumn leaf, asleep on the floor of the little bow-topped wagon we share. Her face was puffy and tears had etched through her white stage make-up. She was still wearing her sequinned costume and a few stars glimmered dimly in her matted hair. She'd clapped her hands together and tucked them under her cheek for a pillow.

Belle must have sensed I'd woken because her eyes pinged open and, without a word, she climbed up the steps into our wooden box-bed and held me. After what felt like ages of teardrops splatting on my head, she shuffled down the bed so we were face-to-face.

 16

"That was *so* stupid, Tansy. You could have died!" she said, her eyes blazing. She choked back a sob, then climbed back down and left, slamming the wagon door furiously behind her.

"A mee-raculous eescape!" Mrs Fratellini shrieked when she heard I'd come round. She rushed to my bedside, her eyes all smudgy, like when you rub something out with an old rubber.

She put the ripped silks on display with the words MIRACULOUS ESCAPE painted on a board, which Boris helped her write. Clowns are often the smartest; you have to be clever to act so stupid. She thought it'd thrill the customers to see that I had clung on and torn a giant hole in the fabric. Now, whenever I pass, I stroke the frayed edges with my fingertips and wonder at the strangeness of it. The silks saved me, yet I can't remember holding on to them.

When I realised I'd never fly again, I told Belle I wished I'd died. Belle said she'd kill me if I ever said that again, but that's because she couldn't understand how much I love flying. Once, when I was little, she made me a kaleidoscope; I played with it for hours, making endless stained-glass snowflakes and wishing I could live in its world. But one day curiosity got the better of me and I took it apart, until all I had in my hands was cardboard and mirror and beads. Belle taped it up, but it was never the same; one by one all the beads fell out, until all that was left was an empty circle of reflected nothingness. Flying trapeze was like living in that kaleidoscope before I broke it; before I broke me.

But I did mend. Mostly, although I couldn't fully raise my arm. It's been three years since I fell; time for my bones to knit back. It takes more than a strong body to fly though; you need courage too and the truth is, mine's shattered for ever. That's my secret. About a year ago, I was hanging out the washing and I suddenly realised my arm worked fine; it was as good as new. But I'm terrified of heights and I can't admit that. Instead, I let everyone carry on thinking my arm never got better. I really want to tell Belle, but there never seems to be the right moment to say I'm a scaredy-cat, especially when she's so fearless.

Now that my flying days are behind me, I earn my place here by washing and fixing Belle's costumes or selling stuff to punters, and I'm pretty sure Mrs Fratellini only keeps me on because Belle's their biggest star. But even though I'm a nobody, I'm always busy; there's always someone giving me something to scrub, stir, stitch, sweep or shovel up, so I try to keep out of sight, in our bed, reading or sewing. I spend so much time here in bed that I've got myself a new name…

"Bug!"

It's Spinnet. I jump up, dropping my book and scattering peanuts. I clamber down the ladder, stuff my feet in my boots and glance at the watch dangling off the bed-end. It's late; half past eight. I check my fingernails are clean, put my coat on and tie my sweet-baskets around my waist. They're made of wood, so even empty they're like carrying bricks and the ties are too tight. I lock the wagon and scurry down the steps.

It's twilight and the air is fuzzy with woodsmoke. The sky is deepest violet and a few stars are already twinkling. I hurry through the camp, dodging tent pegs and jumping over piles of steaming dung. Horses whinny and spicy scents prickle in my nose, making my mouth water. I stop by a pot bubbling on a fire, but before I can breathe its scent, I hear Spinnet yelling again. She makes butterscotch and raspberry drops, as well as ice cream for the penny licks. Her tent is next to the big top so that the sweet aromas waft towards the queues and advertise my wares. I tumble in just as she's opening her mouth to yell again. When she sees me, she clamps it shut until her lips pinch into a thin, hard line.

"The punters are inside already!" she hisses, hammering a slab of butterscotch. A splinter skitters my way and I sneak it into my mouth.

"I was mending Belle's wings," I mumble. Spinnet tuts and loops the Glowbells on the arm I call "my good arm".

"Anyone can sell. It's not like it takes a special talent," she snaps. "You should remember how lucky you are!"

I wish people would stop saying that. I *know* how lucky I am. I only broke my clavicle, ulna, radius, patella, fibula, ankle, two ribs, a thumb and a tiny bone called a trapezium, which I was excited about because I thought it was special to me, until Belle told me that everyone has one in their wrist. Spinnet piles butterscotch into my baskets, glancing at the ties pinching my waist.

"Are they a bit tight?" Her voice is treacly with fake sympathy. I count a beat; I know what's coming. "Well ... that's what you get for showing off!" Spinnet always tries to needle me about my biggest mistake, but when I don't reply, she sniffs and starts packing gooseberry ice cream into the penny licks.

Spinnet used to perform with the silks, but when Mr Fratellini reinvented his circus with an insect theme, he gave her slot to Belle and me. Now, when she's not making sweets, she's a funambulist – a tightrope walker – and a good one, tottering across the high wire dressed as a Black Widow spider, her costume stuffed for a pot-bellied spidery look. She prides herself on being as skinny as a burnt match, but no one would know under all that padding. I'm sure that's why she's always in a bad mood.

"I counted them!" she warns, as she loads the ice cream on my tray and loops the straps over my head. I can only nod; my teeth are glued together with butterscotch.

I pull my hood up and go outside. Spinnet's right; only a few stragglers are waiting to go in, and by the looks of their Sunday-best clothes, they all bought cheap tickets. I doubt they could scrape together enough soldas for a single bag of butterscotch, but I give it a go anyway. I shake my arm, making teardrops of light trickle from my Glowbells.

"Glowbells!" I cry. "Penny licks!"

Not a single punter looks my way. I decide to try my luck inside the main tent and as I edge past, a little boy tugs his mum's sleeve. She catches my eye but quickly looks away; she's got no money for treats. The Mainlanders visit Gala not just for its dozens of circuses, but also for its clean air; for a healthy break from Scoria's factories and the black smog that blots out the sun. But it comes at a high price, and not only for the mum's purse; her skin has a raw, pink look to it and she reeks of carbolic soap. They are very strict about hygiene at the Pleasure Isle ports. She must have had to scrub and scrub to get herself clean enough for Gala. The little boy has the same polished look but the dad's different; the bad air of Scoria is so ingrained in him that even the whites of his eyes are stained with splodges of reddish-brown, like chaffinch eggs. I feel sorry for them, living in that filth, breathing coal-ash instead of air. The little boy tugs her sleeve again, so as I pass I pretend to trip. A bag of butterscotch hops out of one of my baskets and lands by his feet.

"Can't sell it now," I tell him as I kneel down on the damp ground and push the bag into his hands.

He stares at me, open-mouthed, his eyes widening. He slowly reaches out with one finger and very gently prods my cheek.

"Are you Snow White?" he whispers in awe.

Hair as black as night, lips as red as rubies and skin as white as snow.

I laugh and pull back my hood a little so he can see.

"Wrong colour hair." I smile and open the bag of

butterscotch for him. The little boy smiles back and stuffs a lump in his mouth, then I pop the bit he offers me into my mouth. His parents are too busy squabbling above our heads to notice us chatting.

"Well, we're here now," the mum says, nipping her lips together and staring ahead, as if not looking at her husband will stop him complaining. I brush my knees and stand up.

"So expensive," he grumbles. "Could've seen the freaks for half the price!"

"The Butterfly Circus is a *proper* circus!" she hisses back. "They'd never have stuff like that. Looking at those ... those ... poor deformed *creatures*. It's disgusting!"

"Human nature to gawp," the husband mumbles before suddenly noticing me. "Got any freaks here?" he asks under his breath, nudging me in the side. "Apart from you, I mean."

He grins at his wife to see if she thinks he's funny, but her back stiffens with embarrassment. The other punters have heard though and turn to see what he's laughing at.

Belle says I'm remarkable and I love the colour of my skin, the constellation of freckles across my forehead, my forget-me-not eyes. The only thing I get fed

23

up with is not being able to be in the sun much and losing my glasses all the time. But I hate moments like this, when people stare. That's why I always wear a hood. It's not just to keep the sun off my skin; it helps me hide.

But there's no hiding from this one and he fixes his gaze on me again. I wish the ground would swallow me up.

"So what are you, then? An albino or— Ow! What d'you do that for?"

The woman pretends she hasn't just elbowed him in the ribs and I act like I didn't hear him anyway. Slipping away through the canvas door, I work my way along the first-class seats, selling the penny licks so I can collect the empties on the way back. In fifteen minutes I've sold the lot, just in time to see Belle before she goes onstage. When I reach her tent, I feel a twinge of disappointment that she's already in her costume. She knows I like helping her to get ready, but recently she's stopped waiting. I miss tying the ribbons of her satin shoes around her legs or dusting tiny tin-foil stars into the inky night-time of her hair. She's wearing a leotard embroidered with thousands of seed pearls that took me weeks to sew on; I still have the needle scratches on my fingertips. She's sitting hunched over, doing her breathing exercises. From deep in her chest comes a rattle, like when Spinnet shakes the butterscotch. She glances at me but doesn't get up. I cast my eye over her and notice that one of the sequins on the shoulder strap is dangling. Instinctively I reach for the little tin sewing kit I always keep with me, pull out a needle and cotton and tack the sequin back in place.

"Have you taken your medicine?" I ask as I put the needle away. I've made it my job to remind her; it makes me feel closer to her.

Belle shakes her head, still holding her breath. She does this every night, tentatively inflating her lungs as much as she can so she won't start coughing midflight. Being the star of the show has its downsides: she never gets a day off. I uncork a small green bottle and tip some oil onto a square of muslin. It smells sharp and sweet at once and an old lost memory stirs.

"Will you be all right?" I know it's a pointless question.

"I *have* to be, don't I?" she snaps.

Guilt washes over me and I wish I hadn't even asked. What Belle can't say, but we both know, is if she didn't fly, neither of us would have a place here and no one stays on Gala if they're not with one of the shows. I might survive Scoria, but Belle wouldn't. She has to stay where the air is clean and hot, and the sun shines all day.

She breathes in and out through the muslin, turning the air pepperminty. Then she lays her hand beneath her ribs and cautiously coughs, like she's trying it out for the first time. She has to be careful not to cough too hard, or she'll wake the dragon sleeping deep inside; the bronchitis clogging her lungs.

"Belle!" comes a voice from outside.

It's Matteo, Mrs Fratellini's eldest boy. After my fall he became Belle's catcher while Belle learned my tricks and took my part. I never watch though; I can't bear to when there's still no net to catch my sister and even if there were, the truth is it makes me so sad to see what I can never be again. Matteo pokes his head through the canvas flap.

"Belle, you're late!" He sees me and glowers from beneath his bushy eyebrows. "Oh … *you're* here. Aren't you meant to be helping Spinnet?"

I turn away and roll my eyes. Matteo raises his eyebrows disapprovingly at Belle. "Only performers in here," he says primly as he leaves.

"She's just going," Belle says. "And I'm just coming." She waits until he's definitely out of earshot, then whips around to face me. "D'you want to get me in trouble?" she hisses.

I feel like crying, but instead I start clearing her table for her, putting caps on eyeshadows, tipping hairpins back in jars, spooling up her ribbons.

"Leave it!" she says, watching me in the mirror as she paints purple flicks on the outer corner of her eyes. "Spinnet will be waiting. You don't need to hang around here when I'm getting ready..."

I take my time screwing the lid back on her powder just so I can be near her for a few moments longer, then I hug her goodbye, breathing her in. She breaks free too soon and checks her reflection before rushing out to catch up with Matteo. I follow her to the edge of the ring. Matteo is already up on the platform and beckons her with an irritated flick of his wrist. As her foot touches the ladder I realise we haven't done our good-luck charm. I always like to do it, not just for luck but for old times' sake.

"Belle!" I whisper.

She glances back impatiently. I blow a kiss, but before it reaches her, Matteo calls again. She climbs up and disappears into the Hemisphere. She doesn't even look back. My throat tightens and I swallow hard. I mustn't let her see me cry; it'll only annoy her more.

✳ ✳ ✳

Spinnet is waiting for me in her tent, surrounded by spirals of sugary steam. She looks like she swallowed a wasp.

"Late again, Bug! I'm fed up with you! You're twelve now – old enough to work as hard as the rest of us. If you don't, I'm going to ask for someone else to help!" she threatens.

"No!" I plead. "I sold the lot!" I waggle the empty tray. If she snitches on me, Mrs Fratellini will dock Belle's wages.

"Get rid of this lot and I won't tell the boss," she grumbles, making the tray-straps creak with the piles of butterscotch she's loading on. Now I know how the circus mule feels.

I run back inside the main tent. Boris and Doris are halfway through their act. It's dark in the stalls but there's enough light from all the twinkling Glowbells to see where I'm going. I weave through the aisles, stopping at every tier to sell and soon my pocket's heavy with silver soldas and gold florins. I know by the music and applause when Belle's act begins, and I whistle along; here comes the hiccupping trumpet for her caterpillar climb, then there'll be a lilting piano solo as she spins into a cocoon. That'll build to a peak with a harp joining in as she turns into a butterfly.

Just as the harp begins, a lost florin winks up at me. I can't believe my luck and quickly stoop to pick it up; it'll go in our beer bottle with the rest of the florins we've got hidden in the wagon, along with Belle's map of the islands she once traced from Mr Fratellini's old atlas. Belle calls our stash the "Family Fund". She's only fourteen, but she's got our whole lives planned out; we're going to work here until we're old enough to explore every last island of the archipelago, find our parents and be a proper family again. That's our plan and I can't wait to get on with it.

There ought to be fluttering violins for Belle to start the trapeze, but instead the harpist strums the same chords over and over again; I know the sound of a harp ad-libbing. She should have hatched into a butterfly by now, but instead of rapturous applause there's an odd silence. Maybe I've mistimed it, or maybe she hasn't emerged yet. I slip the florin in my pocket and stand up.

But then the audience begin to clap, uncertainly, like hailstones pattering on a roof. I know that clap too; embarrassed, as if the audience aren't sure what they've just seen. The applause builds anyway until the benches are shaking. I can't help myself; I turn to look.

The silks flap emptily and Belle's nowhere to be seen.

I scan the Hemisphere but she's not tucked away up there either. The spotlights are dancing all over the place and I know that Luca, the stagehand, does it to create a distraction because he doesn't know what's happening either.

Something's not right. I feel a sharp pain, like my heart's pinched itself into a tight ball, the way the woodlice do when I find them in the log pile.

Where are you, Belle?

I have to wriggle through the crowds, now giving a standing ovation, to get to the ring. Matteo is shouting frantically at someone unseen but when a spotlight settles on him, he immediately stands still and proud. A fanfare cues Matteo to start the trapeze and he jumps into his next act. The woman next to me elbows me excitedly, her eyes shining in wonder.

"How did she do that, then? Just disappear into thin air?"

I gape at the fluttering silks, my stomach knotted in fear.

"Magic," I whisper. The show must go on.

3

Lost

We hunt high and low, but Belle has vanished. No one saw anything, not even Matteo. I don't know why Belle hasn't told me where she's gone, but I know she must have a good reason. I know she'll come back. She *must* come back.

That night, I stay up long after the search is called off, after every other fire is damped down and the night air cools. Our wagon is tucked away near the animal pens, so close to the circus fence we can smell the forest, and at night we hear the baby elephants snuffling in their dreams. I sit on the wagon's daisy-painted steps and stoke up the campfire, but I can't stop shivering, despite wearing Belle's cloak. By midnight I'm exhausted by doing nothing but waiting and decide to be practical instead. Belle's going to be famished by the time she returns so I pull a pan from the belly box – the storage box under the wagon – and spend the next hour crying under the cover of slicing onions. I add carrots, tomatoes, basil and pasta to make her favourite, minestrone soup, with a pinch of sugar just in case I cried into the pan. While it simmers over the campfire I busy myself in the wagon, making things just the way she likes it. I shake out the rag-rugs, polish the stove and sort through the muddle of threads I use to mend her costumes. I finish a week's chores in one night, but no amount of tidying brings her back.

Dawn breaks, drenching the world with damp grey dew. I feel so lonely, I have to be near something living. I creep into the elephants' enclosure where they are still fast asleep, gently swaying on their gnarled legs like great ships becalmed at sea. I always come here when I'm sad and it always makes me feel better.

But not this time. Instead I sit down on a straw bale and burst into tears again.

Nearly a week passes, with me waiting and hoping until each night I fall asleep on the wagon's steps. But on the sixth night, long after I've crawled into bed, there's a rap on the wagon door and I'm summoned to Mrs Fratellini's caravan.

It's three times the size of the wagon that Belle and I have lived in all these years and much, much pinker. In the corner, there's a huge glass bowl full of goldfish that are prizes for the coconut shy and, next to this, stands a dressing table littered with powder puffs and perfume and a mirror lit up by rose-coloured lights. Postcards of Sanctuary, Gala's capital city, are stuck around the frame and, nesting along the top edge, are Mrs Fratellini's hairpieces. Matteo and his brothers, Mica and Marcio, are already sitting squashed on her small velvet sofa, but as they've all got biceps as big as cobs of corn, they can't sit neatly side by side. Instead whenever Mica, in the middle, leans back, the other two must sit forward and vice versa. Each time the little sofa creaks unhappily.

Everywhere I look, their father Alfredo gazes back from faded photos. There's Alfredo raising a glass or holding his boys aloft as babies, a surprised yet triumphant look in his eyes, like they were something he unexpectedly won in a raffle. In other pictures, he's in a leotard doing some daring trapeze act, muscles bulging like melons. I don't remember him very well, because he died in one such stunt shortly after he found us, but I can tell from his enormous moustache that he was brave, and from his crinkly eyes that he was kind. He was a catcher, not just in trapeze, but in life too. He saved people from falling; people with no one left to love them or who never found anyone to love at all, or who were lost in a forest, like Belle and me. I wish he were here now almost as much as I wish Belle were. I stare at his wristbands hanging on a hook between the floral teacups Mrs Fratellini collects. After the cups, the main thing I notice is Mrs Fratellini's affection for tassels; they adorn every curtain, cushion and tablecloth.

Mrs Fratellini pours the tea and offers me a cup. Her hair, normally coiffed and fluffy, is bedraggled and dull. She's still in the same pink dressing gown she's worn all week and she shuffles between the fire and the window, looking into one and out of the other, constantly sighing.

"We 'av to face facts, Bug," she says, her eyebrows pinching together. "Belle's moved on."

"All her things are still here," I say, carefully placing my cup on a tasselled coaster. My hand is shaking.

"A rival circus would give her everything she needs," Marcio chimes in. "And pay fifty florins a week."

"Think it could be the Spitzers?" Mica adds.

"More likely the Castellos. They've always been the best for flyers."

"I hear Pickingill's starting up again…"

"Hercules Pickingill was never a circus man," Matteo snorts. "He's a crook and a crackpot!"

"Thought he was a zookeeper?"

"He's trouble…"

"Boys!" Mrs Fratellini shrieks in exasperation, clasping her head. She yanks open her bureau drawer and pulls out a wodge of letters bound with string. She looks at me with soft, sad eyes. "Belle never told you about de offers?"

I shake my head. The sofa creaks as Matteo, Marcio and Mica all crane in to see, frowns of confusion wrinkling their foreheads.

"I didn't want to be de one to tell you, but…" Mrs Fratellini says quietly, laying the letters in my lap. Each one is postmarked with the capital city's emblem of a stripy blue-and-gold circus tent and the word SANCTUARY stamped in gold lettering beneath. All the letters are addressed in the same elegant sloping hand:

The Butterfly Circus
For the attention of Mademoiselle Belle

I gingerly turn over the first envelope as if it's poisonous. On the back of it is a wax seal the colour of a squashed grape. It's broken, but I can still make out a horse with a feather plume fixed to the back of its head; the seal used by Circo Fanque, the biggest circus on the whole of Gala, famous for its Liberty horses. I take a sharp intake of breath, like I used to when I flew, and pull out the letter.

Would you like to fly in the most beautiful circus you'll ever see? A place where a star can shine properly, where you can have anything you want?

I only manage to read the first few lines before I have to stuff the letter back in its envelope. No one speaks for a moment. At last, Mrs Fratellini gently tugs the letter out of my clenched fist and stows them all away.

"Louis Fanque taught Alfredo everything he knew about trapeze. Now he's de greatest ringmaster on Gala. Only a fool would refuse an offer to work in 'is circus. Belle is no fool," Mrs Fratellini says as she caresses a photo of Alfredo, her eyes misty. "My Amati always said you would leave me one day. But I 'ave to accept. I wanted my butterfly to be free. Dat's dat!" She sniffs proudly but her top lip is trembling at Belle's betrayal.

"She would've taken me!" I say quietly. I feel a worrying prickling behind my nose.

"Unless she didn't want you hanging around," Matteo mutters.

The boys look at each other awkwardly.

The prickling gets worse, so I turn away from them and fix my gaze on a picture of Alfredo. I cast my mind back to the night before Belle disappeared. I asked her how many florins we'd got and how long they'd last when we went exploring the islands. I wonder if she already knew then that she was leaving. When she tucked me into bed, was there something in her face I didn't notice? I think about the letter. *Anything you want.* So does that include me? I don't think it does, or else Belle would have told me about the offers.

"You must understand," Mrs Fratellini continues, cupping my cheeks gently between her perfumed hands, "eef we don't blame 'er, nor should you."

"It's just business, Bug," Matteo says.

"But we're losing customers," Mrs Fratellini adds. "And wiv Belle gone, dat'll only get worse." The boys nod in unison.

"Mr and Mrs Wood and all the little Woods were

in last night," Marcio mumbles dejectedly, meaning they didn't sell all the seats. I'd already noticed that the crowds have been getting thinner. It's not just that they can go to other circuses; there's the freak shows too. Mrs Fratellini always says the Butterfly Circus is the stuff of dreams, while the freak shows are the stuff of nightmares. But they *are* cheap.

"It isn't just money, Bug," Mica says, patting my arm to make sure I understand. "You have no guardian … you know what that means."

"But I can work. And I've got money." I think of the beer bottle half full of florins.

"Belle is your *legal* guardian and without her we'll be on the wrong side of the law by keeping you here. We could be fined. Or worse…" Mica looks at his brothers to help him. Together they take a collective breath.

"Bug…"

"There's a place…"

"For children…"

"A special place…"

"A safe place…"

I know where they mean: St Mary's on the other side of the island. It's full of Mainlander children whose parents have sailed across from Scoria and abandoned them there, hoping they'll have a better life on Gala.

"You're dumping me in an orphanage?"

"Darrrling, you *are* an orphan," Mrs Fratellini says gently.

"You don't know that!" I shout. No one knows for certain how Belle and I ended up alone in that forest. All I know for sure is I'd know for sure if my parents were dead. I'd feel it in my bones.

Mrs Fratellini can't meet my eye. "I'm so sorry, darrrling," she whispers, but I don't know if she's talking to the photo of Alfredo or me.

I turn back to the picture. Alfredo's face begins to bulge and quiver, but I will not blink. If I blink I'll knock my tears out and I won't let them see me cry.

"Marcio will take you in de morning," Mrs Fratellini says quietly. "Go and pack your things, darrrling, I'll be over in a minute to 'elp you."

4

And Found

It's nearly midnight when I leave Mrs Fratellini's caravan: the witching hour. Swirls of stars speckle the night sky and bats flit across a huge blue moon. The campfires have dwindled to embers and no one's about; there's only my shadow to see me creeping past the wagons. The circus ponies whinny as I hurry by, and the circus dogs stir in their sleep, their green eyes shining in the gloom. I call their names to hush them, but they won't quit their grumbling. Even old Kizzy, the half-blind whippet, growls at me and, when I kneel to pet her, she shrinks back and whimpers. The animals must have a touch of moon-madness.

I scramble up the steps and slide the key in the wagon door. It's as black as a rook inside and I pat the darkness until I find the matchbox and light the candle. I hitch my rucksack off the nail, but I don't know what to pack. Things I need, like clothes and books? Or things I want, like the family of pine-cone hedgehogs Belle made me last Found Day?

"Just de *essentials*," Mrs Fratellini had said as I left. I pack the hedgehogs.

Our box bed is built at the end of the wagon, wall to wall, and decorated with brightly painted birds and gold-edged garlands. I climb up, crawl across the quilt to check the shelf where we keep the map and our secret bottle of florins. Instead, my hand falls on something cold and round that's rolled into the corner.

Something that changes *everything*.

Belle's precious Glowbell. She never wears it during a performance, but she'd never leave it behind. I cradle it in the palm of my hand. It's not just any Glowbell; it's attached to a gold chain rather than a coloured ribbon. It's made of crystal, not glass, and the light from the beads blazes brighter than fireflies. And most importantly, although neither of us remember much before Alfredo found us, Belle was certain the Glowbell was given to her by our mum.

"On my birthday," she said one night as I fell asleep, spinning it until droplets of light flickered on her face.

"We were in a boat ... and you were crying."

"What boat? Why was I crying?"

But Belle didn't have all the answers.

Now I know I was right. Belle didn't choose to leave: she's in trouble.

My head's in turmoil. I'm so happy that she didn't abandon me, but also ashamed that I thought she could. Then both feelings are swept away by a surge of terror. If she wasn't lured away, it means that she's been *kidnapped*. Louis Fanque must have realised flattery was getting him nowhere and decided to steal her instead. I should tell someone, but who would believe me? Mrs Fratellini thinks the world of the Fanques; the two old circus families go back generations. No, it's up to me to find his circus and rescue Belle.

Any second now, Mrs Fratellini will be banging on the door. I loop the Glowbell around my neck and throw Belle's cloak over my shoulders. Then, I stuff the box of matches, the map and the bottle of florins into my bag, and pack them down with my thickest jersey and spare glasses. Then I lock up, slip the key in the belly box under the wagon and slink away through the animal pens.

Circo Fanque is in Sanctuary, which is miles away,

but I know how to get there. I'm going to follow the path through the forest until I reach the old bridge over the ravine. There are some steps on the other side that lead down to the railway tracks below. If I follow the tracks, I can't go wrong.

I scramble over the high wooden fence and drop to the other side. In my hurry I slip and slice my knee open on a rock. It starts bleeding so I lick it clean; it's not wise to have the smell of blood on you when walking through a forest full of wolves. I tear a strip off my shirt and bandage my leg, then stand up and take a deep gulp of outlawed air. I'm on the wrong side of the circus fence at night, on the edge of a dark forest – the forest where Alfredo Fratellini found us all those years ago, when he was out collecting pine sap to make rosin. I shiver with excitement and fear too; Mrs Fratellini doesn't like me out after dark, especially after that night one of our tigers escaped. I shake the thought away; some memories are best left forgotten.

I pull out the map. Under the light of the moon, I check which way to go then run off into the trees. Light sprinkles out from the Glowbell as it bounces on its chain and I'm glad I'm wearing it.

Suddenly, the clouds cape the moon and only the chalky white path is visible ahead, curling like an elephant tusk through the forest. I hear a gentle rustling behind me, but it's only moon-thistles; their fluffy white buds popping open in the moonshine. I stop running and listen harder, beyond the reach of my ear, then I turn slowly on the spot, trying to see something I sense doesn't want to be seen. I wish the moon would come out again.

"Hello?" I call. Only my echo replies, then a deep, dark silence.

I peer through the gloom. Further up the track, I spot the narrow stone bridge that spans from one side of a gorge to the other, where I can see the steps cut into the cliff all the way down to the railway line far below. I hate that bridge, not just because its stones are as wobbly as old teeth, but because Belle once told me a story about it being haunted by a witch. But I'm going to have to cross it.

Just then there's a soft rumbling in the distance. I run up the path until I reach the bridge, where I stop to catch my breath. The bridge is arched with two low walls either side, not much higher than my knee. For a second, I think I spy a movement in the trees, but it must be shadows playing tricks on me. I hesitate, then the clouds shiver away and moonlight floods the stones; so white, like someone threw a glass of milk onto them. I take heart and sprint across the bridge, but I'm only halfway over when a howl rings out. Marcio told me wolves smell humans a mile off and in my mind's eye I imagine one stepping out of the shadows with blood-specked saliva dripping off its fangs. My heart thumps so hard I'm sure I can hear it knocking on my ribs. Keeping a safe distance from the wall, I peer over it at the silvery rails below. They stretch far into the distance before disappearing into the foggy dark of the deep ravine. It's nearly one hundred miles to Sanctuary and I realise it's going to take me at least a week to walk there.

"What are you doing?" I whisper to myself.

The rumbling sound is getting louder. In the distance there's a tiny bead of light; a train is coming. I've made a terrible mistake. I could be gobbled up by wolves or a train could smash me to smithereens down there on the tracks, and no one would ever know. How will Belle be rescued if I'm the only one who knows she's been kidnapped? I'm twelve, I'm scared and I don't want to be on my own. I suddenly remember Belle telling me the witch only comes for naughty children who run away.

I quickly turn back the way I came ... or try to.

I can't move. Not an inch. My feet are glued to the

spot. I feel a terrible fear, not the fear of being out alone at night, but something worse: the feeling that I'm *not* alone, that something is behind me, watching me. I can hardly bear to do it but, very slowly, I look over my shoulder. I breathe a sigh of relief; there's just an empty bridge with nothing there. But if no one's there…

…Then why can I hear breathing?

Soft, so soft, like someone tiptoed right up behind me. There's a damp sensation on the back of my neck. I want to scream, but my throat's frozen stiff.

Pull yourself together.

I force myself to turn around. There's nothing; no wolves, no witch, just my shadow lying across the white stones. Then the strangest thing happens: I feel myself being pulled towards the wall. Without meaning to, I have already taken a step towards it. I try to pull back; there's no way I'm going near the edge. The wall is too low and there's a forty-foot drop to the tracks below.

But the tugging continues and, even though this sounds crazy, it suddenly feels as though my shadow is pulling me. Maybe I hit my head when I fell? I'm sure I'm imagining things when there's another sharp tug, so hard that I stumble into the wall. That's when I hear the ripping sound, like the sound of a cotton sheet being torn. I look down at my feet.

There's a rip where my shadow joins my right foot and it grows, as if a seam is coming undone. I watch transfixed as my shadow tears away from my foot, as easily as I'd tear a piece of paper. I'm still gaping stupidly when I feel my other foot being pulled. I'm hopping on one leg as, for a second, my shadow and I are caught in a tug of war. There's a final yank, another sound of ripping and the shadow is free. I've been pulling so hard I lose my balance and fall roughly onto the wall. A loose stone skitters off and I can't stop myself looking down: the train is hurtling towards me, so close I can read its metal name plaque on the front:

SANCTUARY EXPRESS

Then everything happens all at once. Suddenly I'm leaning right over the edge of the wall and my shadow is dangling from my right hand. It's unnaturally heavy. This is not what I expected; shouldn't shadows weigh nothing? I feel it start to slip from my grasp.

The bridge shakes as the train thunders underneath,

its deafening clatter making the mortar jump from cracks between the stones. I feel my feet slide away from underneath me as a bank of steam engulfs us. I make one last desperate effort to pull my shadow back, wrapping both hands around the shadow's. But then I realise my mistake. I don't have a grip on my shadow – my shadow has a grip on *me*. Its hand is clenched around mine as soft and strong as silk. I'm being dragged over the wall. The train whistle screeches and I want to scream, but fear has locked up my throat. My world turns upside down and I'm falling again.

5

The Shadow

I open my eyes. It's pitch-black. The smell of sunshine and mice and grass, all rolled into one, prickles my nostrils. I'm buried in deep hay; it's up my nose and my mouth is dusty dry. I try yelling for help, but my throat fills with it and I start gagging instead. I fight upwards through the spikey stems until I can feel cold air on my face.

I wipe the dust off my glasses and look around. I'm in the middle of an open-topped train wagon, with high sides that can drop down to become ramps. Every few seconds a huge clot of sooty steam belches overhead as the train hurtles through the ravine. The wagon is heaped with dunes of hay and I guess I've landed in the bedding for animals. The express must be bringing one of the circuses to Sanctuary. Over the train's whistle I hear the mournful trumpeting of elephants and the roaring of lions as the little wagon rocks from side to side. I grab an iron hook fixed to the wall and pull myself up to get my bearings. Looking above me, snow-capped mountains snag the sky and thousands of stars sparkle like diamonds in the velvet night. I gasp in wonder. The wind shrieks around me, whipping my hair across my face, and I'm so grateful to be alive I gulp mouthfuls of the sweet night air. My shadow – if that's what the strange creature was – has disappeared. Was I really pulled off a bridge onto a speeding train by my own *shadow*? That's impossible.

"Shadows can't do that," I say to myself in a steadying, reasonable voice. A Matteo voice.

"Do what?" A stiff, creaky voice comes from behind me, as if it hasn't been used in years. I peer into the shadows, terrified.

"Who are you?"

"Don't be scared," the voice says, from another corner now.

"I'm not," I answer defiantly.

"You are," it murmurs, soft as an ink-spill seeping into a rug. "Your eyes are leaking."

I quickly brush the tears away and squint hard at

where the voice came from, trying to detect a shape in the dimness. Even though my eyesight's bad, from years of checking the ropes when the big top lights go down, I've got a talent for seeing in poor light and spy a denser patch of black in the corner of the wagon.

"What *are* you?" I whisper in amazement.

"I'm a shadow."

"Shadows can't talk!" I shout, trying to sound braver than I feel.

Two eyes flicker open in the gloom. They are lavender-grey; the colour of mischief at dusk. "Then who are you talking to?" I hear the softest chuckle, quieter than the shuffle of dead leaves caught by a breeze.

Just then, there's a gap between the towering mountains. A slab of moonlight falls into the truck and the shadow steps out of the darkness. She's precisely my height and shape; there's the crumple of a trouser-leg stuffed into a boot and two bobbles on the top of her head, just like mine. She's the sort of shadow I only ever have on the sunniest day or under the brightest moon. She could have been cut with the sharpest scissors from the blackest silk but, apart from her eyes, her features are vague; her mouth and nose are just crinkles.

"How has this happened?" I'm too astonished by her to be scared any more.

"Good question," she replies, "I don't know … maybe it's the moonlight?"

I look up; the moon's so bright and close I could trace its seas with my finger.

"All I know is that you didn't want to be alone. So here I am! Ta-dah!" She flings her skinny arms outwards.

I sink down on the hay. I can't believe I'm talking to my shadow. Belle always teases me for talking to myself; she says it's the first sign of insanity. Is talking to your shadow the second? I pinch myself, just in case this is all a nightmare. But then the shadow speaks again.

"Aren't you glad I'm here?" she asks, sounding slightly hurt. She sits down opposite me, resting her pointy chin on the twin peaks of her knees.

"How come you've never spoken before?" I ask, feeling strangely light-headed. "Shadows are silent – as a rule."

"I don't know about rules! I just try to do exactly what you do."

"Shadows don't *try*!" I laugh. "You just *are*!"

"I try very hard indeed," my shadow sniffs. "Ever

spot a mistake? Go on, test me. Move something, quick as you can," she instructs.

I start waving my arm wildly like I'm drawing scrapping cats with a sparkler. My shadow moves in perfect time with me and doesn't make a single mistake. I have to admit, she's very good. But seeing my shadow unfastened from me feels too odd; it's like losing your footing in the dark. I'll never get used to this.

"Well, we need to get back together," I demand, except I've no idea how we're supposed to do it. Is it like sticking down the flapping sole of a shoe? Would she be better stitched? Or could that hurt her? As I'm thinking about this, my shadow drops to her hands and knees and scuttles over the hay towards me. There's a sudden chill, as if a door to a cellar full of unwanted and forgotten things has been opened.

"Has this ever happened before?" I ask, as she settles down beside me. She's so thin I can actually see stalks of hay pricking through her.

"I don't know," she replies unhelpfully. Her eyes are brighter than before and dark sparks flicker teasingly in their depths. "*Has* this ever happened before?" she laughs.

"Well, I think we'd *both* know if it had. All I know is that you tore away from me!" I huff indignantly, but she doesn't seem to notice my tone and lifts the arm nearest to me, waving it around lazily.

"Well, you're the one not moving in time with me … in fact, you're not moving at all," she says primly, choosing a hay stalk and delicately nibbling the end.

"That's not how it works! Anyway, I was doing just fine until you pulled me off that bridge!" I snap, sitting up as straight as I can while she lolls beside me.

"If we hadn't jumped, we'd have missed the train." She takes the stalk from her mouth and taps the damp end of it on my nose. "So, where are we going?"

"To look for my sister," I tell her, brushing the stalk away. "I need to find her."

"Where is she?"

"In Louis Fanque's circus in Sanctuary," I say. "I think she's been stolen!"

"Stolen?" My shadow props herself up on her elbows, suddenly alert. "Like your bracelet?"

"How do you know about that?" I ask. Even I'd forgotten that.

She's talking about the bracelet Belle made me. It was plaited from scraps of wire with beads threaded on it. I never did find out who took it. It was just before my fall; I'd looped it over the bedpost, but in the morning it'd vanished. My heart flutters at the memory and immediately the shadow ripples from the centre outwards, like a stone thrown in a pond at midnight. If she's real, and I'm still not sure she is, then she's real *magic*; old magic – wild, dark and strange. Magic that knows secrets long lost and forgotten.

"I don't know how I know," she whispers, her eyes brighter than ever. "I just do."

The words are scarcely off her lips when we're suddenly plunged into darkness as the train rushes into a tunnel carved through one of the mountains. The shadow instantly presses as close as she can to me, making my side ice-cold. Her hand entwines with mine, and as the train rattles on and the dark deepens, her fingers tighten. I look for the glint of her eyes, but when I can't find it I realise she must have them screwed tight shut. The wagon's wheels clatter on the tracks and my shadow gives a little squeak, burrowing deeper beneath my cloak, cowering like the circus dogs do in a thunderstorm. I hold my cloak down tight around her.

Soon the air begins to smell of sweet pine again and we burst out of the smoky tunnel into the crisp night. It's still summer but snow always falls in Gala's mountains and a flurry of snowflakes swirl into the wagon, dusting the hay white. Immediately, my shadow springs out from under the cloak and slips up the edge of the wagon, her face tilted to the moon, her mouth stretched open as if she's trying to drink the light.

"Are you scared of the dark?" I ask. If she hears me, she pretends not to and lifts her head proudly so that her nose is in the air. I suddenly realise I know nothing about her. "What's your name?"

"Rosa. It's a flower. It smells pink," she answers. I'm about to correct her, because pink isn't a smell, when I realise I have no idea what a rose smells like because I've never even seen one. They can't grow on Gala; it's too hot in the daytime and the nights are always freezing.

She slides down and starts kicking the hay, bunching it up around me. "You ought to get some sleep," she says. "You look tired."

"Shadows should be used to the dark," I mumble to myself, shaping the hay into pillows, but Rosa's hearing is so good that she hears me over the racket of the train.

"I *am* used to it, because *you're* always in the light!" she retorts.

"But that's how you're made!" I parrot what Belle told me when I was little. "Shadows happen when light is blocked."

"I am *not* a blockage!" Rosa replies indignantly, extending one arm into the moonlight, turning it elegantly for me to view. Then she yawns loudly and flops down, crooking one arm behind her head for a cushion and patting the hay next to her.

"I can't sleep," I say, "I've got too much on my mind."

"So tell me about it," she murmurs sleepily, snuggling down and tucking her knees up against her chest. She's so round and black that she could be a well; so deep I could tell her all my secrets and she'd never fill up.

And suddenly, I am. I'm telling her everything; about Belle and me being found in the forest by Alfredo Fratellini, about how much I love the trapeze, about the fall that should have killed me and the silks that saved me, about how my bad arm isn't the real reason I don't fly the trapeze. Then I tell her how sometimes I think Belle doesn't love me any more and how I'm terrified I've lost her for good. I'm telling Rosa things I thought I'd never tell anyone when I hear a little snort from the hay. I give her a nudge, but she's fast asleep; all my secrets have fallen on deaf ears. I sigh and curl up next to her, pulling the cloak up around her shoulders. Then I close my eyes. The last thing I hear is the soft tooting of Rosa's snores over the rattle of the train.

6

Sanctuary's Grand Station

It's happening again. The nightmare. Belle is telling a story, but I can hardly hear it; I'm so warm and sleepy. She suddenly stops. Her heartbeat quickens. Outside, a scream punctures the dark. Now, Belle is standing by the door, a stick in her hand like she's about to go looking for mushrooms in the forest. I tell her she mustn't open the door. I'm begging her not to go outside. Something bad is on the other side. Something bad is waiting for her.

I wake up sweating and open my eyes to sun-shine. I put my glasses on and look up. The sun is glinting through a glass roof perched on a web of beams, dotted with masses of white doves. Purple and gold bunting – the colours of Sanctuary's flag – flap between enormous marble columns. We're here already: Sanctuary's Grand Station.

I clamber up the hay and peep over the side. The station is huge – bigger than I could have ever imagined it would be – with dozens of trains coming and going, and hundreds of holidaymakers and circus performers bustling about. I gawp in amazement at all the people, the brightly coloured gypsy caravans and kiosks, and the huge arched entranceway with a vast clock above it, flanked with yellow, trumpet-shaped flowers. It's late; I don't know how I slept so long. I slide back to where Rosa is still asleep beneath the cloak, but before I get a chance to wake her, I hear voices outside. A beady eye appears at the side of the wagon where a knot of wood has popped out.

"Well, well, well. What have we here?"

The eye blinks for several seconds before disappearing, only to be replaced by another eye, bleary and bloodshot. A moment later, that eye vanishes too.

"Wake up!" I hiss, kicking the cloak. I scramble over the hay and look through the hole.

On the other side, I see a neat little man in a red uniform, with a fez balanced on his head like an upturned flowerpot. His black moustache is waxed to two points and his eyes shine as bright as the buttons on his jacket. Standing next to him is an old man in a velvet suit, cornflower blue, faded at the elbows and in need of a good clean. Fraying gold braids glint across his chest. He must be a ringmaster. He is standing in the shadow of a huge man in a stripy leotard with muscles like knotted ropes: the circus strongman.

"See this?" says the button-eyed man, jabbing a finger at a brass badge on his fez. The strongman nods gloomily. "What's it say?"

The strongman steps up close and scrutinises the badge. He mouths the letters with a puzzled frown.

"Grud?"

"*Guard!*" the guard snaps. He prods the ringmaster's chest with his pencil. "Didn't want the authorities seeing who you're sneaking in, *did* you, Sarrasani?" He thumps the side of the wagon. "Get this open!" he barks.

"The bolt's jammed." Mr Sarrasani shrugs.

The guard looks pointedly at an enamel sign screwed into one of the marble columns.

LICENSED
ENTERTAINERS
ONLY

He licks his pencil and pulls a notebook from his top pocket. "You know the rules," he mutters. "The fine for smuggling performers in is three hundred florins!"

By now a small crowd has gathered by the wagon, craning to see what all the fuss is about. I grit my teeth; I'm trapped.

"Should have guessed a rag-and-bone show like yours would try to cut corners!" the guard grumbles.

"I swear I didn't know she was in there!" protests Mr Sarrasani, stepping up to the wagon and looking in again. I only just manage to scramble back as his mottled eye presses to the hole. "Besides, who'd pay to look at her?"

"Description," the guard continues, elbowing old Sarrasani out of the way and scrutinising me. "Female. Small. White. *Very* white!" His eye disappears and his moustache arrives at the knothole. "You're so pale," he tells me, like I hadn't noticed. "Are you ill?"

Belle says there's nothing more dangerous than a Stupid with a badge, so I clamp my lips shut. He raps his pencil on the wagon, the same way Mrs Fratellini taps the goldfish bowl to get the fish's attention when she's talking to them.

"Where are your parents?" he shouts, the way I've heard Stupids shout at foreigners when they can't speak their language. The moustache disappears; it's safe to look through the hole again.

"Runaway orphan," he concludes, grinding his pencil to make a full stop and snapping his notebook shut. "I've wasted enough time," he grumbles and tries the bolt again but it still won't budge. I hitch my bag over my head and scramble over to Rosa.

"Rosa!" I hiss, pulling the cloak off.

My heart flips. She's not there.

For a second I wonder if when I slept everything went back to how it should be. Wrong can sometimes be slept back to right. I close my eyes and step onto a patch of sunlit hay, praying Rosa will spill out from my feet, willing her to be my shadow the way she used to be, the way she ought to be. I open my eyes and look down: there's just empty yellow hay. For the first time in my life I'm properly alone. First I lose my sister, now I lose my shadow! I squint into the corners of the wagon, wondering if she's hiding. The men are hammering at the bolt. That's when I hear the gentle giggling.

There's a drape of deep black in the shadows where the wagon walls meet. Rosa is hanging from the bolt, stopping the men from opening it on the other side. One of her eyes disappears for a second and I realise she just winked at me.

"I'll hang on a bit longer. Get ready!" She giggles again.

I tie my cloak back on and peep through the spyhole again. Mr Sarrasani and the guard are tugging on the handles, while the strongman tries pushing the bolt in the opposite direction to Rosa, sweat pouring from his brow.

"Ready?" Rosa whispers.

"For what?"

Rosa doesn't answer. Instead she twitches slightly at the very ends of her feet, like a cat's tail, flicking before it pounces.

"Now!"

She lets go and springs away. Immediately the bolt shoots back. The ramp slams down, knocking the men off their feet as an avalanche of hay pours over them. Rosa grabs my hand and, under the slew of dust and hay, we tumble down the ramp and plunge into the crowd.

"Catch that girl!" the guard bellows. He's the first to scramble back to his feet, but he doesn't seem to have seen Rosa. No one does.

A tourist in a floral shirt, unbuttoned to reveal a thick carpet of chest hair, shouts, "Thief!" and lunges for me, but he trips over his luggage. The guard blows his whistle again, but I'm far enough ahead for people not to realise his whistle is for me. We slip in between a waddle of black-and-white robed nuns and just about keep up with them, hiding behind their cloaks. We make it to the end of the platform. There's a turnstile with a depressed-looking ticket collector, pale as a limp stick of celery. I realise that without a ticket we can't get through. I hear the whistle again and look over my shoulder to see the guard thundering towards us, his face as purple as pickled beetroot. I'm trapped between two vegetables.

"In here!" Rosa giggles, pulling me into an empty compartment of a passenger train waiting nearby.

"There's nothing funny about this!" I shout, jumping after her.

"Isn't being chased fun?" Rosa asks innocently. "This way!" She laughs and opens the opposite door. She reaches over to a door on the train next to the one we're on, opens it and hops neatly from one train onto the other. I leap after her and land in the middle of a family who have just unpacked their picnic. They are so busy squabbling over who wants what, they can't have noticed Rosa, but I'm more obvious; I knock ginger beer and sandwiches everywhere and shout "Sorry!" about a million times. The family stop quarrelling with each other and unite to shout at me instead, just as the train shudders into life.

"Quick!" Rosa chirps, pulling me out onto the platform. The train whistles as I slam the door shut. At that exact moment I see the guard, stuck in the first train, shaking his fist at me through the flickering windows as the second train shunts slowly past. His mouth is making ugly shapes around uglier words. It takes me a couple of seconds before I notice I'm not looking at him at all. I'm gazing at my own reflection and I'm grinning from ear to ear.

"Told you!" Rosa whispers in my ear.

7

Les éléphants intelligents

We run hand in hand down the deserted platform, slippery with spilt ice cream and drinks, but then I see there is a second turnstile. It's either the same ticket collector or Celery Stick has a twin, because there's an identical man punching holes in small pieces of card. I skid to a halt, wondering how to escape, when I catch sight of a yellow sign:

**ALL ANIMALS
DISINFECTED
HERE**

We veer right and run up to the marble walls, keeping within the shadows until we reach a gated tunnel.

Crouching behind a heap of fat mail sacks marked for Scoria, we watch as a stubble-chinned porter hauls the wooden gates open. The stench of chlorine hits us. A moment later there's loud trumpeting and three Indian elephants, led by Sarrasani's strongman, sway their way towards the tunnel. Their huge flanks are painted with beautiful swirls of blue and gold, and the word Sercus picked out in orange. They really should have let their clown do the lettering.

"We'll sneak out with them!" I say.

Rosa tightens her grip on my hand and I feel her tense. Just as the elephants trudge past, the middle one hesitates. She's an old lady; her trunk, blotched pink with age, quivers slightly in our direction.

"*Allez!*" I whisper.

I've lived next to circus elephants long enough to learn every order the bullhands use with them; I can ask them to shift a heavy bale for me or shush them when they chatter too late at night. Elephants always know what you want them to do, like the night Belle and I woke in a wagon full of smoke and they arrived to put the fire out, their trunks already full of water. They understood the single note Belle whistled; that's how smart they are. This one knows *exactly* what I said, but it's not *me* who's stirred her curiosity. Her amber eye rolls with interest towards Rosa crouching behind me and I wonder if she can see her. The very tip of her trunk trembles inquisitively and she lifts it in a sort of greeting, then knocks an enormous mail bag out of the way to investigate.

"Oi, you!" bellows the strongman, spotting me hiding. He drops the elephants' leash and rushes at me. "You owe us three hundred florins!"

Rosa grabs the huge mail sack and hurls it upwards. A blizzard of postcards and letters fills the air and the strongman disappears from sight. The elephants trumpet excitedly, then bump against him, almost as if they're trying to stop him catching us. We dodge past and into the dark tunnel, where a pool of disinfectant stretches between its walls. But before we can take another step, there's a pitiful wail. Rosa grabs me tightly in the blackness.

"Hop on!" I shout.

In a flash she's on my back. My knees buckle; it's like she's made of lead. Her arms are squeezing my neck and I can hardly breathe, let alone tell her to loosen up. Instead I let her strangle me as I splash towards the light. I stagger out of the tunnel, wheezing, my eyes stinging from the chlorine and the bright sun. I wipe my glasses clear and see we're surrounded by high bars. We're in the enclosure where the animals' ear tags are checked to see that they're licensed before they're allowed out into Sanctuary.

"Oh, that's better!" Rosa says, like she's arrived at a garden party, slipping down and smoothing herself out. Her blackness blossoms in the sunshine until she's as glossy as blackcurrants.

"No, this is *terrible!*" I snap, wincing as the sunlight hits my skin. I pull her towards a small, shadowy archway, we scamper up some steps and find ourselves in the station entrance hall. We're hit by a wave of noise and colour, surrounded by a confusion of kiosks and caravans; this is where Sanctuary's circuses catch their trade as it arrives. Ticket touts and street performers throng to free the holidaymakers from their hard-won florins. Sweet traders sell from long trestle tables covered in lollipops, toffee apples, bottles of sweets and mounds of chocolate.

"That way!" Rosa points to an arched entranceway. Now that we're close enough to the clock, I see that instead of numbers, there are paintings around the face: different circuses, a helter-skelter, a Ferris wheel, a pier and a pair of theatre masks; one happy face, one sad. The clock hands are hammered out of etched brass, inlaid with purple and green enamel to look like peacock feathers. One of the feathers settles on the pier and there's a spurt of sparks as a bell jangles. The holidaymakers slow their ice-cream-licking to hear better as a metallic voice crackles out from one of the flowers.

"Take a peer from the pier!" says the tinny voice.

Just then the guard's whistle cuts through again. I look back. He's waving his fist furiously at me as he pushes through the turnstile, followed by Celery Stick. The street hawkers instantly pack up their trinket-stuffed suitcases and scram.

"Bye!" warbles Rosa, waving sweetly. I snatch her arm down, pulling her under the toffee-apple table and we scramble along in the dark towards the opposite end. I wait a moment, then poke my head out.

The guard has vanished. Between us and the exit stand dozens of caravans pulled by ponies and donkeys, all offering rides down to the seashore. The nearest caravan to us is painted the colour of fireworks, with a beautiful dappled cob standing patiently between the shafts. In each wheel, gilded spokes beam out from hubs embossed with zodiac signs. Cross-legged on the caravan's footboard sits a hunched-up woman, as wrinkled and freckled as an old Cox apple, wrapped in a ratty green shawl. She's stroking a crystal ball in a theatrical way to attract customers. A fortune teller. I have a hazy memory that there used to be one at the Butterfly Circus, but Mrs Fratellini said she wasn't very good because she never knew about the tiger. Whatever *that* means.

The guard reappears and blows his whistle. The old lady must be there without a licence, because she quickly grabs the pony's reins. My eyes land on the caravan's belly box and I wonder if it's big enough for Rosa and me to escape in.

Before we can move, Celery Stick runs past, checking under the caravans. I pull Rosa under the next stall, hung with garlands of pink marshmallows. We squat in the gloom and spilt icing sugar, keeping watch, waiting for our moment. Suddenly a huge red shoe crashes down next to me and I look up. A twenty-foot-tall man, wearing long striped trousers, a top hat and a spangled waistcoat, lopes over our heads and into the crowds. He's a Peggar – a stilt walker who sells circus tickets. Dozens more throng through the archway like a herd of giraffes, their wooden feet clacking on the polished marble floor as they jostle for trade, baskets of lollies hooked over their spindly arms to lure children.

Now's our chance.

We clamber out from the stall, skidding across the floor, but then the caravan wheels start to whirl as the old lady flicks a whip and the horse trots off obediently. The guard blows his whistle again and I see him lurching towards us, dodging in and out of the Peggars' candy-striped legs. There's nowhere left to run.

Orphanage, here I come. I'm sorry, Belle.

But then, with a grimace of determination, the old lady pulls on the reins and leaps down. She whips her crystal ball out from her shawl and, with an unexpectedly nimble knee-drop, bowls it expertly into the line of Peggars. She hits the central Peggar and he rocks, first one way, then the next, flailing wildly as he tries to keep his balance, snatching at the sleeves of the Peggars around him. Suddenly, all the Peggars are reeling, taking swipes at each other as they try not to fall. But it's too late and they go down like a line of skittles.

The last thing I see of the guard before he disappears beneath the log pile of Peggars is his fez somersaulting through the air. I grab Rosa and we run pell-mell towards the entranceway, leaping over broken stilts and crushed baskets, crunching lollipops beneath our feet. I look behind to wave thanks to the fortune teller but she is nowhere to be seen.

We race out into a cobbled street, its polished stones sparkling in the searing afternoon sun. I have no idea where to go, but we need to move fast.

"I have to get out of the sun," I tell Rosa. "It burns my skin." I pull up my hood and we run into a little park enclosed with high hedges of silverberry. Children are playing hide-and-seek around a pool with a fountain of three tumbling clowns, and families are waiting with their luggage, writing last-minute "Wish you were here" messages on picture postcards before they go home. The bottom of the pool has disappeared beneath a layer of glittering stars. Nearby, other children are feeding silver soldas into the coin slot of a metal monkey that says, "How do you do?" in a scratchy voice, before doffing its cap to reveal a tin star balanced on a brass plate underneath. Even wishes cost money in Sanctuary.

I spy a little hollow in the bushes – a fox run, and the perfect place to catch my breath. I back into it and crouch down out of sight and out of the bright sun. I quickly scan the park to see if the guard followed us, but he's nowhere to be seen.

"Are we playing hide-and-seek too?" Rosa asks happily, squishing in next to me.

"This isn't a game, Rosa!" I hiss. "If they catch me, they'll put me in an orphanage!"

I'm hot and frightened. Even if I did start enjoying myself back there for a moment, I didn't mean to. I've got a job to do; a sister to find.

 73

"What's an orphanage?" Rosa asks, idly plucking a leaf from the bush. She looks like she's not listening, but I tell her anyway. I like being the person who explains things for a change.

"It's a place full of children."

"Full of children?" she says, watching the families with interest. "Sounds fun."

"It isn't," I correct her sharply. "It's a prison for kids without mums and dads."

"So, you don't have a mum and dad?" Rosa rips the leaf from its spine so that she's left holding a teeny fish skeleton in her hand.

"Of course I do!" I snap. "I just ... don't know where they are."

The only time I asked Mrs Fratellini about them, she burst into tears and ran from the room. She thinks they're dead, but she's wrong. I know they're out there somewhere, still looking for Belle and me. One day we'll be a proper family again.

"What about Belle? Can't you share her mum and dad?"

"We did share, that's the whole point!" I puff. "How can my sister have a mum and dad if I don't?"

"What is a mum and dad exactly?" Rosa asks lightly, busy making a playmate for her first fish.

"Well…" I start, trying to picture my mum and dad, so Rosa will understand how important they are. But no matter how hard I try, I can't see them, I can't even conjure up their faces.

Rosa turns to me expectantly. "Yes?"

"Well…" I keep my voice steady and flat, just like Matteo does when he explains something to Belle or me. Or Mrs Fratellini. Or Spinnet. "Mums and dads look after you." I sigh. It'd be lovely to have a mum and a dad to look after me and Belle; bet they wouldn't make me do chores all the time.

"I see." Rosa nods firmly like that cleared everything up for her.

I breathe a sigh of relief that she didn't want any more details, and decide to use short sentences more often. I realise I have lots of questions about shadows too. Are they born? If they are, is Rosa's mum my mum's shadow? But I'm giving myself a headache, so I stop.

"Let's go," I say.

Rosa drops the fish and grabs my hand. In the bright sun she glitters like coal and I hesitate, looking at the crowds around us. "Can people see you? Would they be scared?"

"I think they only see what they *expect* to see." Rosa

shrugs. "Except maybe small children. They haven't learned what they should expect to see so they still see everything."

I lift up my cloak to drape it over her anyway.

"Better safe than sorry."

8

Funicular

We keep running until we reach a clifftop and the sparkling blue sea filling the horizon as far as I can see. In front of us is a wide, breezy walkway enclosed with wrought iron railings to stop people pitching over the edge.

"Oh!" gasps Rosa, rushing ahead. "It's lovely!"

I force a smile and hold on to the railings, taking slow breaths to stop the collywobbles in my tummy. We're sickeningly high up – higher than the birds – but the view is so beautiful, it almost makes me forget my vertigo. From here I can see most of the Pleasure Isles, the lush green mountains of Flora and Fauna and the snowy peaks of Jambor. If I leaned out further I'm sure I could see Popina too, but I'm too dizzy for that. These are the islands that Belle has shown me so many times on the map; the islands that we are going to explore together one day. The thought of that makes my skin tingle and I wish that Belle were here with me, seeing them for the first time together as we'd always planned.

Sanctuary spreads out below us, just like in the picture postcards I saw pinned up in Mrs Fratellini's caravan. The town is split down the centre by a long flight of stone steps that zigzag down through the old cobbled streets. There must be close to a thousand steps until they reach the bottom of the cliffs, where a long, spindly pier pokes out far into the channel between Gala and mainland Scoria, a great smudge on the horizon, shrouded in smog. At the very end of the pier sits an old theatre; a large white building, fancy as a wedding cake and topped with turquoise, onion-shaped domes. Out at sea, paddle steamers are churning the blue waters white and in their wake, schools of dolphins are leaping in the surf. At the other end of the bay there's a shamble of faded buildings, a boarded-up playhouse and a vast helter-skelter, taller than a church, painted to look like a lighthouse. Beyond them, away from the tourist spots, is the municipal dump. There, Sanctuary's rubbish is loaded into garbage-boats and taken back to the mainland, where the authorities say it's too late to matter any more.

From up here, I realise that the blue-slate roofs of the houses spell SANCTUARY in block letters, readable from the sea and possibly even Scoria. Closer to the shore, where the ground levels out, there are gardens with bandstands and boating lakes where tourists can row in swan-shaped wooden boats. In the corner of the two main parks stand the biggest circuses, the golden finials of their big tops glowing. Waltz music tinkles upwards as if someone far away flipped the lids of many music boxes at once. But the place that has really made my heart beat faster is two hundred feet below me. It's five times the size of the Butterfly Circus, with three big tops and foil bunting shimmering between the king poles that reads:

CIRCO FANQUE

For the first time since I set out to rescue my sister, I wonder if I'm doing the right thing. Maybe Belle doesn't *want* to be found. She probably has a luxury caravan of her own, a feather bed to herself, where she doesn't get kicked all night long, and no money troubles to worry about. *No one* to worry about. Matteo's words scratch in my mind: *Unless she didn't want you hanging around.* My throat tightens with sadness, but then I feel the weight of Belle's Glowbell resting on my chest. I'm certain Belle wouldn't have left this behind if she'd gone willingly. I pull Rosa towards the steps.

"Quick! It won't take long," I lie, grabbing the handrail. The white-washed stairs stretch ahead like a keyboard, octave after octave. It'll take us ages to reach the bottom. Rosa peers distastefully down the stairway, her bottom lip sticking out.

"I don't like walking," she grumbles, plonking herself down on the top step. "I don't have the right sort of toes." She lifts a foot onto her lap and strokes it gently. As far as I can see, she doesn't have any toes at all; her legs just look like a pair of floppy tights.

"It'll be fun!" I use the voice Mrs Fratellini adopts when she wants me to pick up poop in the elephants' paddock, but Rosa just scowls and settles down further. I remember how when I was little, I'd try to slide my shadow under a door and it would never work. I'm just about to tell her off for being stubborn when I hear a clanging. Hidden behind a clump of blue-blossomed hydrangea flowers, something glints. I squint and see what looks like a sparkling red double-decker tram with a line of tasselled parasols along the top deck. A sign next to it reads:

FUNICULAR

"What's that?" asks Rosa following my gaze.

"It's like a train that goes up and down a cliff."

"How does it get down there?"

I point to the bottom, where another carriage is about to start its ascent. "The weight of this one pulls that one up."

The driver finishes ringing the bell and slumps in his seat, elbows resting on his paunch, gazing through the gritty windscreen. We scurry up the steps.

"Oi! Where you going?" he snaps, prodding the rock towards a sign:

1 TOUR = 1 FLORIN

"Nice tan!" He laughs, looking me up and down.

I shove a florin in the slot and a purple ticket pops out.

"Only kidding, love," he says, as I glower at him. His cheeks turn red as he clips a hole in the paper and

I try to remember what Belle told me once. *Just because people say unkind things, doesn't mean they're unkind people.* There's no one else on the tram, but I still clamber up to the top deck anyway, where I'll be less obvious. Rosa settles on the seat opposite, basking in the full sun like a seal on a rock, watching me with interest while I fight to open a parasol.

"You've changed colour," she observes enviously. "I'd love to change colour. It's boring always being plain old black."

"I'm hot," I lie. It's too hard to explain that I'm not embarrassed about being pale, but about his comment. "Anyway, you do change a bit," I say, trying to make her feel better. "Before you were purple-black, but in this light you're kind of dark grey."

She crosses her arms sulkily. "I'm never grey," she retorts and turns away, ignoring me. The tram judders into life and the doors slam shut. I'm just about to say sorry when I realise Rosa is happily swinging her legs again, all slights forgotten already.

We lean back in our seats as the carriage creaks down past the pretty houses we saw from above, each one with window boxes to match; blush peonies for pink houses, cornflowers for the blue ones. This has to be the most colour coordinated place I've ever seen, although that's not saying much; the Butterfly Circus has been my whole world for the past seven years. As I look out across the blue-slate roofs of the houses and the sparkling sea of the bay, I wish more than ever that Belle were sitting next to me to see it too.

"Does your sister look like you?" Rosa asks sweetly, craning her neck to see.

I haven't had any breakfast and my tummy's rumbling. I'm so hungry I feel a pinch of annoyance that she can be so cheery.

"Of course we look the same. We're sisters."

Spinnet often says she can't believe Belle and I are even related, because my hair is orange and hers is black, my eyes are blue and hers are brown, I'm short and she's tall. But I only notice how we are more alike than different; we have the same frizzy curls, the same upturned nose, the same smile, the same laugh. Our eyebrows have little dragon-tail flicks at their ends and we can both roll our tongues. And if someone didn't notice all that, then we each have a dimple on our cheek; Belle's is on her left, mine on the right. Anyway, just because people look different doesn't mean they don't belong to each other.

"She'll be easy to spot then," Rosa says.

Just then my stomach growls again.

"D'you hear that?" she whispers, panicked. Before I can stop her, she drops down to her knees, hiding under the seats.

"It's me!" I drag her back up to my side. Her eyes have widened to the size of Mrs Fratellini's teacups and are the colour of spring violets.

"You can talk from your *insides*?"

"It's not talking. I'm hungry. I need to eat."

"Why didn't you say?"

She digs her hand down into a sort of gap in her side, like an invisible pocket, and drops a garland of marshmallows in my lap. Without stopping to think where she got them, I cram five in my mouth at once. They're delicious.

"Bear-bib-boo-bep-beeze-bom?" I mumble, spraying her with icing sugar. I already know the answer.

"The station," she answers innocently. I swallow the marshmallows down and wipe the sugar off my face. It's uncomfortable telling someone off for stealing when you've got their stolen goods smeared over your chin.

"You can't take stuff without paying, Rosa!"

"*You* did."

"When?"

"*You* just took five from me."

"That's different," I say. "We're sort of … we're like … we're like two parts of the same person," I explain. It's the first time I've thought of us this way. I turn to see if she understands and find her deep in thought, twisting her fingers through a loose tendril of her hair.

"But we've torn apart…" she whispers, gazing over the slate roofs. "What if you lose me?" We're nearly at the bottom and the funicular is slowing down.

"I won't lose you!" I grab her hand and hold it tight. Even though she's right next to me, she feels very far away.

"You lose lots of things."

"What are you talking about?"

Rosa sits up very straight. "You lost your mum and dad … you lost your bracelet, now you've lost your sister." She shrugs helplessly. "I'm just a shadow. I'd be even easier to lose … especially in the *dark*." She trembles.

I open my mouth to explain but before I can, the carriage suddenly jolts to a stop.

"C'mon!" I say, squeezing her hand. "I promise I won't." And together, we climb down the steps.

9

Circo Fanque

The wide promenade is lined with orange trees, the beach on one side, Sanctuary on the other. Street lighters are out on their stilts, lighting the candles in the lanterns swinging between the trees. Sanctuary's days are short and hot, its nights long and chilly.

Hawkers and tinkers, with trays of tin toys and souvenirs hung from their necks, weave through the throngs of holidaymakers. Children run by, blowing bubbles through clay whistles. Street performers juggle or scam holidaymakers with card-play. I'd love to explore all of this with Belle and I feel a pang in my chest as I wonder where she is. There are dozens of food stalls along the seafront, and Sanctuary's salty air thickens with their scents. There are signs everywhere, advertising chocolate churros, toffee-coated chestnuts, fire-breads loaded with smoked meat, burritos running with melted cheese and Sanctuary's speciality: roasted cockles. Mrs Fratellini once told me that no one wastes time going to restaurants in Sanctuary and if it's fancy food you're after, you'd be better off on the Isle of Popina, where restaurants serve risotto made with white truffles and cherry ice cream flecked with edible gold.

We slip into the crowds heading towards Fanque's big top, which glows in the distance. It's lit up by hundreds of painted paper lanterns hanging off glittering poles that lead up to the entrance. Strains of organ music drift out from behind the crimson-and-silver canvas; the evening performance has already begun. I leave Rosa waiting by a curly iron gate into one of Sanctuary's many parks and race up to the small kiosk, where a freshly pasted poster advertises a new trapeze act. Inside the kiosk a woman with spirals of golden hair gazes out at the passing crowds, chewing gum and filing her long lacquered nails into spear shapes.

"So who's the new star?" I ask as casually as my fluttering heart will let me.

"Wouldn't want to spoil the surprise." The woman smiles. "Ticket?"

"Just one," I say, slapping my florins down on the counter. Even the cheapest seats cost four times as much as the Butterfly Circus. The woman frowns.

"You can't *buy* one tonight. They sold out weeks ago!" She lets her gaze linger on my sleep-frizzed hair and stained cloak. "And *cheap* seats sold out months ago."

"But I've got to get in!"

"Sorry, lovey." She nudges the florins back at me with the tips of her talons.

"What about tomorrow?"

She flips through a calendar and grimaces. "One ticket, month after next." She shrugs. "Ask your mum and dad to bring you back next year." She turns back to filing her nails.

"No!" I snap, pushing the florins back again. "I need to get in tonight!"

"I told you – there are no tickets." She's stopped chewing and glares at me. "Beat it, kid!"

"I'm not going anywhere. I want to speak to your boss!"

"Louis? He's a busy man."

"Yes, he is! Busy kidnapping star acts from other circuses!"

The woman snorts and waves me to one side, but

I stand my ground. A few passers-by slow in order to listen in. Normally I don't like the attention, but this is exactly what I need. I push my hood back and a few more people dawdle as they pass, looking at me and my whiteness with curiosity, listening to our row. That's fine by me – I want them to know why I'm here.

"That's right, you heard me," I say, raising my voice even louder. "Louis Fanque kidnapped my sister!"

The woman starts laughing but there's a dangerous glint in her eye. "Louis? A kidnapper?"

She's still laughing when her arm darts out. She wraps her talons around the scruff of my cloak and yanks me up over the counter, lifting me off the ground.

"Look here, Snowdrop," she hisses. "I don't know who sent you to bad-mouth Louis on the busiest night of the year, but I can guess, and I'm telling you it didn't work last time and it won't work this time. So scram or I'll set the dogs on you!"

She lets me go and I fall backwards. A second later she pops her head out of the kiosk to watch me sprawl around on the ground. "And by the way, he's not my boss. Louis is my husband."

Just then a family race up, out of breath. I stare enviously as the father pulls out their gold-edged tickets and they slip inside the big top. As the tent flap is held open for them, I glimpse a huge oval ring, surrounded by scarlet and gold curtains embroidered with tigers, dragons, flying horses and peacocks. Seats, covered with midnight blue silk, are tiered in order of their price, with the most expensive ringside places cornered off by golden rope. Spotlights flicker across the Hemisphere, where the spangled equipment rocks gently in the breeze. I strain for a glimpse of Belle, but then the flap is dropped back as the stagehands tie it down.

"Let's try round the back!" Rosa whispers, her breath damp in my ear. She tugs me towards the performers' caravans nestled behind the big top and we creep around, looking for a stage door. The circus walls are sheets of overlapping canvas that have been laced tightly together and we inspect each one carefully, but with no luck.

"It's impossible!" I wail. "We'll never get in."

"*You* can't," Rosa says. "But *I* can!"

In the blink of an eye, her knees suddenly bend back to front the wrong way and her legs slide towards the canvas, slithering along the ground like two eels. Then the rest of her follows and she vanishes from sight under the tent. So she *can* slide under doors after all!

"It's dark!" comes a muffled voice. There's a rustle as the ropes keeping the flaps of the tent together start being undone. Finally, Rosa's hands wriggle out and she pulls the flaps open enough for me to climb through. "Quickly!"

I scramble inside. We're in the clown alley. Elephant drums, tinsel-coated hoops, walking globes, diabolos and devil sticks are stacked ready for the show. A clown arrives to trundle out a wheelbarrow and we duck down. Rosa clutches my hand tightly in the dark.

"Hold on to my cloak," I tell her as we step into the crowded auditorium. "We've got to keep out of sight!"

We duck beneath the banquette, the wooden fence around the ring, then crawl under the tiers of seats, creeping across hundreds of little skulls of stale popcorn, through forests of legs and mountains of coats. I can smell rats and every so often something warm and scratchy slithers across my outspread fingers. A fanfare announces the next act and the seating above me rocks as the audience stamp their feet in time to the circus elephants tramping tail to trunk around the ring, while the band plays.

At last we reach the main spotlights. I crawl out from under the seats and pull Rosa up behind me onto a small wooden platform, where the huge lights are so close above us that I can feel heat blaze on my head. The instant the last elephant stomps out through the tasselled curtains, a lady trots into the centre of the ring wearing a red-and-black riding jacket. She's carrying a long whip, which she cracks twice, making blizzards of sawdust. Immediately a white horse prances into the ring, followed by nine more, each with gold painted hooves and purple plumes standing stiffly from their polls. They pick their way delicately around the ring, lifting their knees as high as their shoulders. This is the act Louis is really known for.

"Oooh!" coos Rosa. "Dancing horses!"

"They're not dancing," I correct her. "They're liberty horses…" My voice peters out; Rosa is too happy being dazzled to listen. The horses canter around the ring, kicking up a surf of sawdust. They are riderless except for the last horse, which has a woman in a too-plain leotard balanced on its back. As she passes I suddenly smell something perfume-sweet.

"Can you smell honey?" I ask, but Rosa's too transfixed to answer. I follow her gaze and see a globe of something quivering, gold and black, lowered down on a rope from the rigging above. I rub my glasses clean with my finger and squint harder. That's when I hear the angry buzzing. The glistening ball is shifting with thousands of tiny velveteen bodies crawling over each other. The woman rides by and the first few bees follow the scent and settle on her waist. Steel hoops are lowered into the ring and she leaps through them, now followed by the entire swarm, curling behind her like the fiery tail of a dragon. Out of the blue I remember Matteo undoing the magic of this infamous trick by explaining it: the swarm are helplessly lured by the queen bee, locked in a tiny cage sewn to the woman's belt. There's a fanfare and a jangle of cymbals. The horses canter out to rapturous applause.

"That was amazing!" gasps Rosa, her eyes bright as sapphires.

"Seen better," I mutter, determined to be unimpressed.

"Where?" asks Rosa eagerly.

I scowl at the ring and fold my arms in case I start clapping despite myself. The lights are cut. As usual, I know what's next: the Carpet Clowns while another act prepares. I look up, searching for Belle. Ladders disappear into the shadowy heavens and the rigging gleams overhead. As soon as I blink out the dazzle of the spotlights, I see them. Dark shapes are climbing up the *corde lisse* towards the performers' pedestals. It could be the tightrope walkers getting ready for the high wire, but then I spot a trapeze being slung from one platform to the next.

My heart starts racing. I scan the Hemisphere. Then I see one of the ladders tremble and I track back down the rungs to where it disappears behind the ring-door curtains for the performers. There's a triangle of light where the curtain has been lifted to let the stagehands through and I spot a movement. Someone wearing sparkly tights is dabbing their feet into a tray of rosin before climbing up the ladder.

I'd know those skinny legs anywhere.

10

Spectacles and Surprises

The clowns take their bow and the lights are cut once more. Any minute now the aerial acts will start. A spotlight dances around the auditorium, settling first on a man gorging chocolate, then a boy stealing a kiss from his girlfriend. Everybody laughs. The light skitters around, looking for its next victim. I pull Rosa back under the seats. Her eyes glow like a cat's.

"I'll get lost!"

"You won't!"

I grab a tight hold of her hand and we sneak back under the seats again, scrambling through the darkness until we reach the performers' entrance. We squeeze out through a missing board of the staging, then sneak behind the giant velvet curtain. I look around for Belle, but all that's left are her footprints in the rosin tray and I catch the scent of a forest. A forgotten memory begins to bubble up, but then the rope ladder trembles and I see movement among the rigging. My heart sinks; she must be in the Hemisphere already and just gazing up at it makes me sweat.

The spotlight returns to the centre of the ring and a little man, wiry as a coat hanger, strides into its beam, waving and clapping. Louis Fanque himself, ringmaster and owner of the largest circus on all of Gala, wearing the tallest top hat I've ever seen.

"He looks happy," Rosa says cheerfully.

"He should be," I say. "He's making a fortune stealing other circuses' acts." The band strikes up and Louis drops a low bow.

"Ladeeze and gentlemeeen," he croons. "Boys and gurrrls…"

I look up again. Two sparkly legs are dangling over one of the halfway platforms. It's Belle. How have they made her do this? They must have threatened her. I feel a wave of anger and hatred for Louis. I'm going to make him pay.

"Belle?" I whisper, but she's too high up to hear me.

"Tonight we have a *spectacular* new act for you…!" Louis smiles with too many teeth.

"It's me, Tansy!" I hiss, louder now. I take a deep breath and dab my feet in the rosin, squishing out Belle's footprints; smaller than I remembered. I grab the ladder and step on the first rung. The rope creaks and a wave of giddiness washes over me.

"Oooh! Are you joining in?" Rosa giggles.

"Just keep a look out for me!"

She rolls the black flaps of her hands into a binocular shape and diligently peers through, scanning all around. I begin the climb.

Don't look down.

"For the first time ever...!" Louis continues.

Another rung, a seventh, an eighth. I'm ten feet up – the highest I've been since I fell.

Don't look down.

"On the Isle of Gala..."

A ninth, a tenth, an eleventh. The ladder wobbles horribly; my stomach somersaults.

Breathe. Don't look down.

I grit my teeth and climb another three rungs, my heart thumping like a drum. Belle has started climbing higher but she's always slower than me. If I'm quick, I can reach her before the act starts and help her escape. Together we can do this.

I swallow hard and climb up again. The Hemisphere's

dark is thicker than normal dark, and the air up here smells different from the rest of the circus: sharper, more dangerous. I stop for a moment to collect my breath, to quell the giddiness. Far below, Louis is now just a red blur to me, like a squashed ladybird in the middle of the white ring. There's a slow drum roll.

"Circo Fanque's latest attraction. The amazing, the lovely…"

My eyes have got accustomed to the gloom and I can just make out the silhouettes of the artistes waiting on the other landing boards. I check to see Belle's progress: she's pulling herself onto the tinselly platform to take her bow. I force myself to climb higher until she's within my grasp.

"Our very own Bell—"

She's not your Belle, Mr Fanque. She's mine.

I stretch out and wrap my sweaty fingers around the nearest sparkly ankle. I'm met with a squeal of angry surprise.

"—issimo Beatrice!"

Bellissimo Beatrice isn't quite so lovely with her face contorted in anger. She glares down at me and kicks my hand away, yelling in a language I don't know. Someone below hisses at me. I forget about not looking down and suddenly I'm frozen, stuck on the ladder.

Meanwhile, Bellissimo Beatrice has kept her cool. Hats off to her professionalism; she acts as if everything's wonderful, like a weird girl *hasn't* just snuck up the ladder and grabbed her. She waves brightly to the crowd. She's perfection; her wide blue eyes in a heart-shaped face and Cupid's bow lips stretched into a smile. She looks nothing like Belle.

I suddenly feel a damp chill.

"People see what they expect to see *and* what they want to see," whispers Rosa. She's clinging to the underside of the ladder. I never even felt her climb up.

"I can't get down," I croak.

"I was wondering how you got *up*..." she replies. "With your *bad* arm."

She stares at me intensely for a moment more, then lightly places her hand over mine. "Close your eyes."

Very gently she moves my left hand down a rung, followed by my right foot. Then again and again. Slowly but surely she guides me down the ladder. The whole time she hums a little tune through her nose that I recognise but don't know the words to. That's what I concentrate on; not the angry shouting from below.

We're only just on the ground when a finger and thumb has me in an expert ear pinch. It's the stage-hand from earlier; he's wearing saggy trousers held up by braces and his peach-fuzz moustache says he's only a little older than me.

"Look who it is – Miss Snowy!" His breath is hot against my cheek. "Saw you snoopin' around earlier!"

I wriggle like a ferret but his grip is firm; if he twists my ear much harder he'll rip it off. But then there's a twang and he lets go. His trousers collapse to the floor and he scrabbles to hold them up, hopping from foot to foot, trying to cover himself with one hand and pull the trousers back up with the other.

"Whoopsie-daisy!" Rosa snickers in my ear.

We charge further backstage, past acrobats limbering up, a strongman with two men balanced on each shoulder, and a woman spinning from a bar clenched between her brilliant white teeth, flashing with the diamonds embedded in them. We dive to the right to avoid her and smash through a juggling family, all dressed in identical sparkling red outfits. They hurl their gold batons after us, but by then we've skipped onto a heap of lion-tamer's drums and down the other side. Without warning, Rosa drops to the ground and slides under the tent flap. I try to follow, even though I know the gap's too small, dropping to my knees and shoving my arms under the canvas, my face against the damp earth.

"Pull me out!"

"Aye aye cap'n!" Rosa yells, yanking me under the canvas with the strength of a gorilla.

"Hurry!" I hiss.

"Heave-ho!" Rosa laughs.

I'm halfway out when someone grabs my ankles.

"Gotcha!"

It's the stagehand again. I kick back with all my might but he isn't letting go and Rosa's hands slither out of my grip as I'm dragged back into the tent. I only have time to whisper, *"Wait for me!"* before I'm lifted to my feet.

"It's the kid I saw earlier, boss," says the stage-hand. He turns me around and suddenly I'm facing the crook himself, the great Louis Fanque, all five foot nothing of him.

"Where's my sister, Belle?" I shout, lashing out with a bunched fist. The stagehand grabs my wrist.

"You!" Louis gasps, a smile breaking across his face. "The little trapezist from the Butterfly Circus! You broke your arm, no?" Without taking his eyes off me, he yells over his shoulder, "Sophia! Quick! Come and meet one of the all-time greats!"

All-time greats? I don't know what his game is, but his silver tongue isn't fooling me.

"Where's my sister?" I demand as the kiosk lady emerges from behind a tent flap and glowers at me.

"She and her sister are the best trapezists on Gala…" Louis says, beaming.

"We've met," the woman mutters. "She thinks you've been doing a bit of kidnapping, sweetheart."

"Is that so?" Louis chuckles, gesturing around the troupe that have gathered to see what all the commotion is. "Yes, most of my artistes have to be forced to perform in the greatest show on Gala," he finishes, cocking an eyebrow at me, his eyes full of gentle mirth. The strongman roars with laughter and my cheeks flush.

"Her face, like a white rose in morning sun!" Louis whispers to Sophia.

He's *such* a smooth-talker! I break free of the stage-hand's grip.

"I saw the letters you wrote to Belle! You snatched her! She's here, isn't she?" I stare him down, but instead of looking upset, he shakes his head in bewilderment.

"Maybe you saw them, but you obviously didn't *read* them. If you had, you'd know I asked if—" he leans in closer, peering intently at me— "*you* would come too."

"W–what?" I stammer.

"The Fratellinis are like family to me, but business

is business. Yes, I wrote to Belle – she's your guardian after all – but I thought I could persuade you *both* to join us. I thought there might come a time when you were fully mended and could fly for me. However, your sister's very loyal to the Fratellinis and refused all offers." Louis's brown eyes hide no secrets.

I'm confused. Why is he talking about me performing again? I might have been somebody once, but those days are over. Belle's the star, the one everyone wants.

"She must be here," I whisper, tears tingling behind my eyes.

Louis pats me on the shoulder. "I'm sorry."

The troupe give me a pitying look. If Belle's not here, then where is she? I feel like something inside me has crumpled and my eyes well up. I hear the soft shuffle as everyone except Louis and Sophia melt away, protecting me from my own embarrassment.

"I really am sorry," Louis says, glancing over his shoulder. He's due to go back in the ring to announce the next act.

"So, where else could she be?"

He shrugs helplessly. "No real circus would ever force someone to perform…" He frowns. "But you could try the old playhouse."

"Pickingill's place?" Sophia asks, laying her hand

103

on his arm. Her eyes widen as the crease between them deepens.

"She's old enough to handle herself. She got all the way here, didn't she?" Louis smiles, looking me over.

He tugs a picture postcard from where it's been stuffed in the edge of a dressing-room mirror. It shows a map of Sanctuary and its main attractions, including the pier and the funicular. He taps his finger on a pair of theatre masks close to the huge helter-skelter we saw from the clifftop.

"You can't miss it." He hands me the postcard and I stow it in my pocket. Then he struts back to the ring. "Remember," he says, glancing at my arm, "my door's always open to you." He gestures towards the Hemisphere above.

Sophia starts undoing the cords in the tent wall. "Listen, kiddo," she whispers. "That place isn't safe. It's falling apart and Pickingill's a nasty piece of work. Not the kind you mess with. He's not *real* circus – he's a sideshow man. They play by different rules." She loosens the last cords. "Go home and get those lazy Fratellini boys to come and flex some muscle. Don't go snooping around that playhouse alone. You're just the kind of act Pickingill would like. You'll be asking for trouble."

She holds the canvas open and pushes me out, so quickly I don't have a chance to tell her that she doesn't need to worry. Louis was right; I can handle myself. And besides, I won't be alone.

11

Pickingill's Marvellous Mechanical Machines

The canvas flaps shut behind me and I step out into the chilly night air.

"Rosa!" I whisper. A little hiccupping sob is coming from the bushes where Rosa is now waiting under one of the lanterns. The flame has burnt low and she's standing in its small circle of light, cowering from the encroaching gloom. At the sound of my voice she leaps towards me.

"Where did you go?" she cries.

I pull her into a hug but she feels so chilly against my chest, I quickly let her go. "Sorry, but I've got a clue where Belle might be!"

I grab her hand, leading her towards the park. Rosa hangs back, peeping over my shoulder at the darkness.

 107

"The moon's out!" I assure her, but she won't budge. I know what she wants. "Come on," I say, and a second later I'm stumbling under her lead-like weight as she jumps on my back again.

I lumber through the park's gates, past hedges shaped to look like seals with spinning balls on their noses and ladies pirouetting on horseback. Crooked shadows fall on the ground and the grass is dotted with dusk-daisies. I'm trying to keep to the patches of moonlight so Rosa feels safe, when it suddenly gets even gloomier. Even I can barely see, and I'm used to the dark.

"I don't like this!" Rosa squeals, tightening her grip around my shoulders, squeezing the last scraps of air out of my lungs. I hear panic in her voice and the last thing we need is panic. I panicked that night the tiger escaped and I still panic every time I have the nightmare. I remember Belle telling me to count every forget-me-not embroidered on our quilt, divide the number by four and times it by three. Now I realise what Belle was doing. I need to distract Rosa.

"If only I could see Polaris," I gasp.

"Polly who?" Rosa replies with interest. Her grip loosens a little.

"The North Star. It's a big bright one. It'd help me navigate."

She points ahead. "Is that it?"

"Nope," I say, stumbling between two yew hedges.

"That one?"

"No, keep looking," I wheeze.

Rosa sees another eight stars before she spies the real North Star, by which time she's forgotten why she's hunting for it, or that she was scared of the dark. She starts whistling the same tune she hummed when I got stuck up the rope ladder. I'm trying to remember where I know it from when suddenly I spy a weather-vane up ahead, adorned with theatre masks. It must be the playhouse. I stagger through the park gates, into a gloomy street winding between tall, narrow houses; their black-slate roofs hunched over their eaves like raven's wings.

"Off you get!"

Rosa reluctantly slides down, but keeps close by my side. This corner of Sanctuary feels forlorn and forgotten. Shop windows are full of left-behind summers; dog-eared postcards and paper windmills blanketed with dust. A sign creaks above my head, but whatever it advertised has been sun-bleached, leaving nothing but a smiling mouth, floating on a vanished face.

We turn the corner and the old playhouse looms in front of us. It's made of creamy stone and the doorway is domed with three arched windows above it. Over the windows is a curved piece of whiter stone emblazoned with EMPIRE, except that the "R" and the "E" have worn away. My heart sinks as I see that every single door has been securely boarded up, but we creep up the crumbly steps to take a closer look. As I peek through a chink in the boards, the stale scent of greasepaint and old leather hits my nostrils. I listen to the blackness inside, trying to detect any sound that might be Belle, but my ears are met by silence.

"She's not here," Rosa says too quickly.

"We need to check inside," I tell her.

I pull at one of the boards and we squeeze through. I strike a match and it flickers in the damp air in a blaze of yellow. We're in a small foyer, with a plush red carpet and thick wallpaper peeling away from the walls.

"I can't hear anything."

"Good!" says Rosa. "Let's go then."

"We can't! Louis said she might be here. I *have* to check!"

We tiptoe to a counter with doors either side marked EXIT and ENTRANCE. I rattle the handle to the entrance and crouch down to squint through the keyhole. "I can't see anything. The key's in the lock…" The match sputters out and instantly Rosa clings to me.

"Now can we go?" she begs.

I light another match and this time unhook a lamp from the wall and light it.

"I'm not going to lose you, Rosa!" I tell her, patting her back gently. "But I have to get that key. Belle could be a prisoner in there."

I take out the postcard Louis gave me and slide it under the door, then pull a hairgrip from my hair and poke it in the keyhole. There's a clatter as the key lands and when I pull the postcard back, the key's on top of it. As soon as I slip the key in the lock, the mechanism turns and I shunt the door open against its rusted hinges.

Thick cobwebs stretch across the gloom like threads of glue. As I brush them away, I suddenly see a figure lurking in the shadows, standing sentry to a dark tunnel. He's seven feet tall and dressed in a black velvet cloak and a top hat. The heels of his boots have steel spurs, which start twirling, sending streams of sparks into the air like miniature Catherine wheels. The giant turns towards us, but before I can run, Rosa grabs my arm.

"Don't worry," she says. "It's not real!"

She reaches out and gently prods the figure to show me. Overhead, a wire glints from the door to the giant's head; it's more than a puppet, it's an automaton, a mechanical man-made man. Its brass face had been painted with a moustache and red russet cheeks, but the paint's peeling off. The green glass eyes are set in two cavities, so ill-fitting they rattle as they flicker in their loose sockets. As its chin drops, I realise the automaton is trying to speak, but the mouth keeps jamming until, at last, it jolts down and hangs limp. A thick-legged spider scuttles out of it as it speaks.

"Svell-com … svell-com … svell…"

Frightened, Rosa lashes out, landing a vicious right hook under its chin, snapping the mouth shut again. Instantly, its arms spring outwards, holding a banner that reads:

Pickingill's Marvellous Mechanical Machines

The automaton's head slumps down to its chest and its arms snap back. Our fright over, we scurry past Pickingill's automaton towards a long passage lined with glass cases, each with a chrome panel and coin slot. The first three are empty and the only clue as to what automatons were exhibited there are strange titles like "The Cat and the Canary" or "The Tiger's Lunch". Only the last booth is occupied, simply called "Interval". A mangy monkey squats inside, wearing a frilly cap, holding a tray of ceramic pies with blackbirds wriggling out from under the lids.

"I don't like it," Rosa says, creeping closer. "It's a *real* monkey," she whispers. "And real birds."

She's right. The monkey is stuffed; the work of a taxidermist and not a very good one judging by the bulging eyes, set so far apart it looks like a hammerhead shark crossed with a chimp. I can see where wires run from its paw into its arm and the tiny springs that make the blackbirds flap.

I shudder and pull Rosa on. The passage makes a sudden U-turn, and ahead are three more booths. In the first is a headless clown, holding a coloured box with the lid enough ajar to see its missing head inside. Then there's a stuffed pig, dressed in ruffles and a pointy hat, next to hoops to somersault through. The last compartment contains a lion tamer, his whip raised against an overstuffed real lion, raising its moth-eaten paw to defend itself. Ahead is the large oak-panelled door marked Exit and underneath, Come Back Soon! We've reached the end of the exhibits and there's no sign of Belle or Pickingill.

I hear the town clock chime midnight and despair beats down on me. My sister is missing; my only lead has gone cold, I'm hungry and tired. I don't know what to do next. If I go back to the Butterfly Circus to get help, I'll only lose even more time.

Rosa senses my hesitation. "It's OK," she says softly. "We'll try again tomorrow. You'll feel better after a sleep." She leads me back past the creepy exhibits until we reach the foyer again, where we shut the door hard behind us. "But let's not sleep here!" she says quickly, looking into the dark corners where shadows are creeping down from the ceiling; where anything could be hiding.

"Everyone's a bit afraid of the dark," I say, squeezing her hand reassuringly. "Even Matteo's scared of giving the ponies their supper unless there's a full moon."

To the right is an archway with STAFF written above it. We go through and find a small room with a fireplace and a basketful of kindling. On the mantelpiece leans a mirror, on which someone has scribbled "Break a leg!" with lipstick; and next to that there's a small heart-shaped pincushion, stuck with pins. Heaped on the floor is a huge bundle of velvet, gold tasselled curtains that must have once hung across a stage.

I rip up some tattered old programmes and light

a fire. Rosa slips down next to me and pulls the curtains up around her like a hen's nest. My tummy gurgles again and Rosa looks at me with interest.

"You're hungry," she says, pleased with herself for hanging on to this detail. I nod sadly. It's too late to get any food now; all the stalls will have shut up for the night.

She reaches into the concealed pocket that I can never see and pulls out a handful of jelly beans, a liquorice snake, three cherry drops and a candy wristwatch, its sugary beads threaded on elastic. She must have snaffled the lot from the station.

"We talked about taking stuff!" I say in my strict voice.

"Help yourself," she chirrups, laying the goods on the curtain between us before snapping the watch over her wrist. "I only want this," she says, stroking it lovingly. She lifts her wrist to her ear and listens intently.

"Rosa," I say firmly.

She ignores me and takes the watch off, shakes it and listens again. I realise there's no point in talking to her about stealing; I'm just going to have to keep an eye on her.

"Shouldn't they tick?" she asks, passing me the watch to examine.

"It's not real," I explain. "It's for eating."

"Oh," she says disappointed. "You keep it then."

Rosa's eye is caught by a little black beetle scurrying across the hearth. Without warning she snatches it between her finger and thumb and swallows it whole. There's no crunch, no chewing. The beetle simply disappears into her mouth as if it tumbled down a drain.

"You like bugs?" I ask, trying not to gag.

"No." She sounds glum.

"Why eat it then?"

"It was black."

"You have to eat black things?"

"I thought it might be good for me." She shrugs. "Put a little colour in my cheeks..." She angles her head for me to observe. Sure enough, her cheeks are beetle-black, full of a dark shine.

"You should have the liquorice then." I suggest.

She tilts her head back and drops the strand neatly in her mouth, like a thrush with a worm. She smacks her lips and nods earnestly.

"Much nicer than the bug!"

"Really?" I say, but Rosa is too busy chewing to notice my sarcasm.

The lamp flame gutters and the dark creeps closer. Rosa slides nearer me, making my sides feel chilly.

"Will the fire go out?" she asks nervously. I poke a twig into the embers and flames flicker up.

"Not 'til you're asleep," I tell her as I settle down. I've only closed my eyes for a few seconds when Rosa squirms.

"Are you asleep?"

I grunt a response that's meant to mean, "Yes" but there's more tossing and turning.

"I'm not sleepy," she says brightly. When I open my eyes I find her face just millimetres from mine. She's studying me hard.

"Shut your eyes and try." I turn onto my back, blinking at the ceiling. It's going to be a long night. "What about a story?" I suggest.

"Or a game?"

"No," I say firmly. I know how boring I sound; only a grown-up would say no to a game. Rosa hunches over miserably, watching the flickering shadows on the wall. Out of the blue, I remember how Belle would look after me when the nightmare woke me up. *Don't cry, little candle, you'll put yourself out*, she'd say. Then she'd reach up behind the bed and pull the Midnight Toy Box off the shelf. It was just an old sugar carton that she'd painted indigo, drawn silver stars on and filled with different toys for me to play with. I think of the hedgehogs in my bag and wonder if Rosa would like one. I rummage in my bag for it.

"What about a midnight toy?" I coax, holding out the littlest hedgehog.

Rosa's so excited, she trembles like a leaf and curls her hand around it, running her fingers over the little pine-cone spines. I snuggle back down into the musty curtains again and shut my eyes, listening to the fire crackling and pretending I'm back in the wagon.

"I was just thinking about my old toy box," I murmur sleepily. "Wish I could remember what happened to it."

"I'll see if I can find it…" Rosa whispers.

I'm trying hard to stay awake but my body is heavy with tiredness. "Huh?" I mumble.

"The memory," she says. "I'll look for it. While you're seeing and thinking and hearing and feeling, I catch your memories that spill over. Memories you forget to remember, memories you don't want to remember…"

At least I think that's what she said. I'm falling asleep … and Rosa talks on through the night, remembering the old and far-flung memories. But I'm too tired to listen properly and drift in and out of her words, like a boat that's broken its mooring; sometimes knocking into a sandbank before being carried back out to sea on the next wave of sleep.

12

Pickingill's Parade

The next morning, I wake up to Rosa shifting in the curtains.

"Listen!" she says and cocks her head to the side. In the distance comes the sound of organ music. "Could be a circus?"

Another circus may mean Belle! I scoop up my bag and the pine-cone hedgehog and stamp my feet back in my boots. Outside, the sun is only just rising and the air is cool and misty, already full of the scent of doughnuts frying. We run back down the street until we reach the furthest end of the promenade, where the strains of the organ are getting louder. There's a buzz of excitement as families gather, pointing at something coming towards us.

 119

A weary young elephant is towing a huge showman's carriage, and kicking up a dust storm from the dry road. She has a distinctive bump in her head, painted with an orange sun. At last she trundles to a stop and waits obediently, rocking from side to side and stamping her enormous feet. She looks so miserable. Her flanks are callused from where the carriage shafts have rubbed her skin. As the clouds of grit settle, the carriage emerges. It's beautiful, with rows of gilded lilies along the top of the high, straight sides, blazing like a crown. On one side, a mechanical organ magically plays without an organist, the notes drifting out from golden pipes. On the other side, in foot-high letters are painted the words:

Pickingill's Cabinet of Curiosities

FEATURING

Miss Pinch

The Fantastic Flying Furball

& other peculiars & notables

ALL NATURAL

And underneath, in smaller print:

Some exhibits may differ from those advertised.

Management cannot be held responsible for any unforeseen changes in attractions, abominations, NOR BE LIABLE FOR deaths incurred or illnesses contracted.

All ticket sales final. Non-refundable. No swapsies.

My heart flips. Could Belle be one of the peculiars and notables? Did Pickingill snatch her for this so-called Cabinet of Curiosities?

Just then, a second wagon arrives with a giant octopus fighting a whale in a stormy sea painted on all sides. It's pulled by another elephant. She has the same little bump in the middle of her head and I realise she's the first elephant's sister. I cast my eye over her; she must be a couple of years younger than the first. She's not much more than a calf and far too small for her load. I feel another surge of anger towards Pickingill. Gripping Rosa's hand, I drag her through the crowds towards the wagon, shoving people out of the way in my hurry. I don't care how many toes I tread on, how many people give me sharp looks and sharper words; nothing matters but finding Belle.

A fanfare erupts and the lilies light up as a bright green tent suddenly bursts out from the roof of the carriage and spirals up into view. A skeletal man appears under the tent, hunched like a three-legged crow as he leans on his ivory cane. This must be Pickingill himself. He's wearing a black velvet suit with coat-tails brushing his ankles and crocodile-skin boots with spurs on the heels that spin of their own accord. I realise the automaton in the playhouse was meant to be him. As the crowd clap his grand entrance, he releases scraggy starlings, one by one, from his pleated silk cravat and they flap into the air. A sausage dog, black as a seal, dances at his feet, snapping at the birds and revealing a set of sharp metal teeth.

"Do you believe in myths, ladies and gentlemen? Do you believe in miracles?" Pickingill yells. "I, the Great Impresario Pickingill, bring you genuine artefacts from the wild. The rarest specimens! Never before seen by human eyes!"

I scan the carriages for any sign of Belle. I feel a strange heat in my head, like fear and anger spun together as every fibre in my body wants to rush up and attack him, but I need to be cleverer than that. While he carries on talking about how great he is, I creep around the side of the second wagon, out of sight from the crowd.

"What are we doing?" whispers Rosa, tiptoeing behind me, her eyes glittering.

I wedge my fingers in the crack between the wagon's panels, but before I can wriggle them apart, Pickingill lifts a silver whistle to his lips and blows. No sound comes out, and I realise it must be too shrill for human ears, but the back doors of his carriage swing open and five tiny acrobats tumble out, dressed in identical black coat tails to Pickingill's, with silky cravats tied tight around their throats. They are capuchin monkeys, the sort I've seen dancing for peanuts on street organs; the clever, crafty ones. To make them look even more like him, Pickingill has dyed their fur black and oiled it flat on their heads with pomade.

"*Regardez!*" Pickingill says, with an elaborate flourish towards the wagon we're standing by. The crowd surge forward with a collective gasp. Two monkeys start cranking an iron handle at the top, making the seascape panels slide apart. I jump away and watch as a huge glass tankful of water is revealed. A hush falls on the crowd and coloured lights flicker on, illuminating the interior.

"Behold Coral! The world's first mermaid in captivity!"

Perched on a rock with her back to us is a small mermaid. If she had legs I guess she'd only reach my hips, but she doesn't; instead she has a snaking silvery fish tail wound around the rock. She tries to comb her long hair but it keeps wafting away in sea-weedy strands. The crowd gasp, but I know it's an old trick. There isn't water in there: it's a line painted around the top of the tank, and then the glass is coloured deep blue to seem like water. I bet some monkey, stashed out of sight, is working a fan to blow her hair about. The mermaid slides off her rock and hides in a drift of seaweed in the corner.

"Is *that* your sister?" Rosa says, gawping at the tank.

Before I can answer her, the elephant turns a beady eye towards us and blinks. She pokes her trunk under my cloak, nosing around. Meanwhile, Rosa has slipped up to the back of the tank, her face pressed up to it.

"She looks scared," she says, peering at the mermaid, "and angry."

The end of the mermaid's tail is poking out of her hidey-hole, swishing back and forth.

"Want to see more?" Pickingill croons. "Get your tickets now! Grand opening next week at Pickingill's Cabinet of Curiosities! Find us at the end of the pier!"

The lights flicker off inside the tank and the capuchins crank the panels shut. The crowd moan but music starts up again and Pickingill blows the whistle again. Immediately the remaining monkeys run into the crowd, shoving circus flyers in pockets and down shirts, snatching ice creams, shrieking as they tear up into the boughs of trees and throw more flyers into the air. Pickingill chortles at the chaos he's created, claps his hands excitedly and kicks his heels together. Up there on the carriage, with the honky-tonk music plinking metallically, he looks like a giant capuchin himself, dancing on a gilded organ.

"Plenty more marvels like Coral! Last few tickets, folks! Once they're gone, they're gone!" He cackles.

It's the oldest technique in the book: tell someone there's only a few left of something that they didn't even know existed and suddenly that's what they want most in the world. The crowd fall for it. They surge up to the carriage, pushing each other in their frenzy to get tickets. In the commotion I didn't notice that Rosa has climbed up the side of the mermaid's wagon and is wheedling her fingers between the wooden panels, trying to prise them apart.

"What are you doing?" I hiss.

"Setting her free!" Rosa answers, as if it's the most obvious thing in the world.

The elephant pokes me harder with her trunk and a deep rumbling sounds from her throat.

"*Tais-toi!*" I whisper, but the little elephant doesn't

like rudeness. I push her away, but elephants are as stubborn as they are strong and she shoves back. I'm trying to keep my balance when I hear a loud crunch: Rosa has wrenched one of the panels open.

"Rosa!" I gasp in disbelief, glancing over to see if Pickingill has heard. The elephant pulling his carriage turns to see what her sister is looking at and they trumpet together, swinging their trunks in excitement.

"Rosa! You're spooking the elephants. I think they can see you!"

"Elephants *like* me!" Rosa trills.

The elephant trumpets louder.

"Tais-toi!" I whisper again. But she won't shut up. Instead she stamps her feet, swinging her trunk to attract the other elephant's attention. Pickingill grabs a long leather *chambrière* from its holster at the top of the carriage and raises it to whip the little elephant. He's just about to crack it down on the poor animal's back when he sees me.

He freezes and gapes in disbelief, the expression in his eyes slowly transforming from anger to hunger. He quickly slides the whip back in its holster and flashes me a winning smile. Making a big show, he digs into his pocket and pulls out a single ticket, which he waves in the air.

"Ladies and gentlemen," he shouts. "Look what I just found! A front-row seat. A VIP backstage pass! Free to one special person!" He pirouettes around, scanning the crowd. "Which one of you is going to be my lucky winner?" The crowd push towards him again, but he doesn't take his eyes off me. "We need to choose that very special someone … you! Little girl!" On cue, the crowd turn and gawp at me. "Come up here and collect your prize!"

The crowd moves in, encircling us. I grab Rosa's hand.

"Up you come! Don't be shy!"

Pickingill blows his whistle again. The capuchins leap down from the wagon and surround me, chattering and shrieking. "Quickly, quickly!" Pickingill shouts and the monkeys grab me, pinching and scratching. I try to jerk away but they are too strong.

"Get off me!" I yell as they drag me towards Pickingill. Quick as a snake, Rosa yanks their tails. The monkeys squeal in terror and scamper back up onto the wagon, quivering with fright.

"No more monkey business!" Rosa giggles as we dive down under the wagon.

"Stop her!" Pickingill yells hysterically.

The crowd has swollen, with more and more people

trying to get the free ticket. They mob Pickingill, thrusting his own flyers up at him for him to autograph, blocking his way down from the carriage.

"Don't let her get away!" he screams, as we duck between the elephant's legs, the capuchins racing after us. Panicked, the elephant rears up in terror, bucking backwards. The wagon shafts snap in two and the elephant breaks free, dragging the splintered wood behind her as she runs off.

"Run!" I yell.

Using the elephant as cover, we sprint off down the street. I run faster than ever before, until blood is thumping in my ears. I can hear the monkeys shrieking behind us but I don't look back. I run until my chest is a ball of pain, until my legs feel numb, until each breath feels like a rip. I'm not running for me; I'm running for Belle.

The elephant charges off down the promenade before disappearing into the park, leaving us exposed. The gang of capuchins spot us and come racing towards us. We nip down a small alley I hadn't noticed before, but when we reach the end, our exit is blocked as a wagon screeches to a standstill. Sitting up on the footboard is an old woman, her shawl flapping in the wind. With a flood of relief I recognise her: she's the fortune teller who rescued us at the train station.

"Quick!" the old lady yells, her eyes wide in fear. "Get in!"

I look back; the capuchins are scampering towards us. I grab Rosa's hand and together we hurtle towards the wagon. Just as I feel the nearest capuchin claw at my ankle, the fortune teller grabs me by the collar and yanks me up onto the footboard.

And that's when I let go.

I don't mean to, but the wagon starts moving and Rosa is so heavy, her hand slips out of mine. I stretch back, trying to reach her but the wagon speeds on and I miss. The howling of the monkeys gets even louder as the fortune teller gees the pony up. Rosa runs alongside.

"Grab my hand!" I yell down to her. I reach for her outstretched hands, even though I know I can't possibly catch her; the wagon is going too fast and our fingertips just brush. "Wait!" I cry, but suddenly the old lady shoves me through the open door behind her seat. I lose my footing and tumble inside. The door slams shut and the caravan hurtles back down the street, tilting crazily as we careen around the corner and back out onto what I guess must be the promenade. I stagger to my feet, crashing from side to side as I try to get back to the door. That's when I hear the sickening sound of a bolt being shunted into place. I'm trapped and Rosa is out there all alone.

"Help!" I yell, as loud as I can. I made Rosa a promise; I said I'd never lose her and now I have, just like she said I would. I bang my fists on the door until my skin stings.

"Shut it!" the fortune teller barks.

The wagon thunders along for what feels like ages until we suddenly hit a bump in the road and I'm thrown back down to the floor. I realise from the sound of the wheels clattering on wood that we must now be on the pier and, noticing a little crack in the door, I press my face against it and peep out. White railings run along either side, with dozens of square kiosks selling penny licks and postcards. Their zinc roofs glitter in the sun, and their windows have flowers etched all around the edges.

There are a few large green posts painted with a white anchor to show the paddle steamers where to moor along the pier and, as we trundle past, I spot a steamer arrive, blazing with red-and-gold carved balconies that curve around her bow. As the latest tourists spill out, I shout for help again, but they're far away and too busy enjoying their first penny licks. Instead they gawp into shadowy tents: the exhibits that have been hidden away in the sunless gaps between the kiosks. Outside, billboards are luridly painted with scenes of a tattooed Snake-Woman with a boa-constrictor, a huge red swan flapping rainbow-feathered wings and a man with a unicorn's horn spiralling from his head. The freak shows; Mrs Fratellini's stuff of nightmares.

Belle told me half these exhibits aren't even real. The red swan is an old hoax: the birds are fed paprika until their feathers turn scarlet. It's just one of the tricks of the hatchet-faced men prowling the pier; the sideshow owners, the wolves. The air is thick with their ugly shouts as they hustle the crowds.

"Ugliest Man in the World. Seeing is believing!"

"World-famous two-headed pig!"

We pass a red-and-yellow-striped tattoo parlour covered with hand-tinted photographs of the tattooist's work: a woman covered in green scales to look like a crocodile, and a man whose face is inked with feathers like an eagle. As we roll by, the tattooist himself steps out, putting his boards up with the new designs on offer. He's an ox of a man, with greying stubble and a bright red bullseye tattooed on his bald head, which seems risky, looking at the gulls flying overhead.

The wagon rumbles to a standstill. We're at the very

end of the pier. Just ahead is the old theatre that Rosa and I saw from the clifftops. Up close, its white plaster has crumbled away. Two tall gates with chipped blue paint and scraps of barbed wire and glass pinned along their tops slowly creak open. The caravan trundles through. I hear the gates groan as they close and the gulls are silenced. We must be inside the building.

The fortune teller clambers down and pulls across a bolt at the back of the wagon. I sneak up close to the door and the second it opens I spring out, straight into the glare of a lantern. A sack is thrown over my head. I try to kick out, but the fortune teller holds my wrists tight in her hard, bony hands.

"Stop struggling," she snaps, pushing me down some steps. There's the sound of a key in a lock and a creak as a door opens. Air as damp and musty as a church hits me and I'm pushed inside.

13

The Trap Room

I scramble to my feet, coughing and spluttering. It's pitch-black and the only clue as to where I am is the smell of greasepaint, seawater and wood-smoke, all mixed together. Beneath the floor I can feel the ocean pounding against the pilings and I realise I must be in a trap room under the stage, where the theatre props are stored.

I'm glad Rosa isn't down here with me; she would hate how dark it is. Here and there, chinks of light stipple the dusty floor, seeping in from the gaps in the stage above. It's too gloomy to see much further than my outstretched hand, so I edge forward, fumbling my way around plywood trees and bushes, a dragon made of canvas, a tarnished suit of armour and a rack of costumes. When my fingers touch something soft and bristly, I nearly scream before realising it's just a stuffed bear, its clawed paw raised in attack. It's stuffed so badly its snarl looks like it's laughing at its own joke. But no sooner than I've breathed a sigh of relief I hear a scuffling in the shadows.

"Hello?" I whisper, wondering for a moment if it could be Rosa. There's no reply. I hold my breath and back away, but before I've taken two steps, my arm's grabbed. I scream and try to pull away but the grip tightens.

"Get off!"

"Tansy?"

It can't be. But it is.

It's Belle, my Belle!

"What are you doing here?" she cries, pulling me into the deepest hug anyone ever got lost in. I'm so happy, I can't even speak. Instead, I hug her back, breathing in her scent, relief surging through me as I feel her heart thud against mine. Suddenly, all the tears I've held back this last week flood out in ragged breaths.

"I've got you!" she murmurs in my ear, the way she used to when the nightmare woke me, squeezing me so tight I can hardly breathe. At last she releases me.

"How did you get here?" she asks.

"I caught a train," I tell her. I don't know how to even start explaining the rest.

"But how did you know Pickingill had taken me?"

"I went to Fanque's because Mrs F said you'd gone there to work and when you weren't there, Mr Fanque said Pickingill might have you, but you weren't at the playhouse either and this morning there was a parade and a mermaid, and Pickingill tried to catch me with his monkeys but his elephants escaped and an old lady tricked me but I—"

"Stop!" Belle says. I take a gulp of air. "Mrs Fratellini said *I'd* gone to Fanque's?"

I nod.

"I'd never leave without you!" she says indignantly before scrunching up her face as she catches up with the truth. "Wait—did *you* think…?"

"She showed me the letters," I say, flushing with the shame of doubting her.

"You know me better than that," she says, her eyes widening with hurt surprise.

"It wasn't just the letters," I say quietly. "You…"

"I *what*?"

The truth is I don't want to tell her the truth. But Belle lifts my chin with her finger so I have no choice.

"Sometimes it's like … you don't want me around,"

135

I say quietly. I wish the truth didn't sound so mean.

"What? I love you…" she starts. Then I hear it; the silent "*but*" she stopped herself from saying. Pools of tears tremble in her eyes as she opens her mouth to explain, but nothing comes out. She looks down at her hands, knotting her fingers together. When she finally speaks again I have to strain to hear her.

"It's because … it's my fault," she whispers. "I let you fall…"

There it is.

My sister's secret; the monster she's been hiding from. Monsters can be just four short words; they don't always wait until nightfall to come out. They can stand right behind you in broad daylight, breathing down your neck all day long. All this time I thought Belle didn't like having me around, but it's just that she felt guilty.

"And you'll never fly again," she finishes, glancing at my arm.

"You didn't let me fall!"

At that exact moment I see my own monster too; I've been so ashamed of being afraid that I lied to the one I love the most. A lie that meant my sister's guilt could grow. A lie that seemed so small to begin with but has cast a long shadow over both of us.

"My arm's better."

"What?"

"I've wanted to tell you for ages."

Belle gazes at me blankly before a slow smile spreads across her face and she laughs with relief. "That's fantastic! You love trapeze!"

I shake my head. "But … I'm scared."

Belle's smile fades as she understands the truth.

"You're *going* to fly again," she says determinedly. "You'll see."

Then she wraps her arms around me and holds me again, and just like that, in a heartbeat it's back to how it always was; as if we've both come home.

"C'mon," she whispers after a few moments and leads me across the room. Behind some scenery is a metal bin with a hole cut into it to make a fireplace. A kettle stands on a wire grill on top of the bin, with tin cans jammed together to make a chimney pipe. Around the fireside is a semicircle of packing cases and trunks. Belle sits me down on one, pokes the embers of the fire and feeds it some sticks. She coughs suddenly and her whole body shudders with the effort. I realise she must have been without her medicine for all this time.

"I'm all right," she says quietly, as if reading my mind. She sits for a while, taking deep steadying breaths while I gently stroke her back.

"What happened that night?" I ask.

"Pickingill was waiting for me," she says. "He grabbed me after my first climb up the silks."

"But everyone could see you up there?"

"It's an old trick! It was a dummy made from a piece of rolled silk. When it unrolls, it looks like the person disappears."

"Someone must have seen?"

Belle shakes her head. "Not in the pitch black. You saw the lights cut out?"

I don't answer. I've not told her I never watch.

"It was just a few seconds, but long enough for Pickingill to make the switch."

I remember the woman nudging me in the ribs, her eyes shining in wonder. "Well, you got a standing ovation," I say.

Belle pulls a face. "The Fratellinis must hate me if they think I just left for money, especially after everything they've done for us."

I feel another twinge of shame. I realise that I've been so busy worrying about how I feel that I never gave too much thought to the Fratellinis.

"She said they didn't blame you ... and neither should I."

"But Sanctuary's such a long way. I'm surprised she

let you travel alone. Since the tiger, she barely lets you out of her sight."

I look down at my lap, but Belle pinches my chin to turn me to face her.

"Tansy!" she gasps. "They'll be worried sick!"

"They were going to put me in an orphanage!" I reply indignantly. "Anyhow, I wasn't alone."

"What?"

I know how crazy this is going to sound and a small voice in my head tells me Belle might be a bit too grown-up to believe in magic. I take a deep breath.

"Can you keep a secret?" I ask.

"Yes…" she answers guardedly.

"My *shadow* helped me!" I whisper. "She kind of … came alive!"

Belle laughs and gives me the same look she used to give me when I'd eaten all the nuts and told her the elephants had wriggled their trunks through our wagon window, unscrewed the nut jar, then put it back neatly again.

"It's true!"

"And is her name Rosa by any chance?"

"How did you know?" I ask, amazed.

She kisses my forehead. "Don't you remember? When you were little, *really* little, you used to talk to your shadow." She hooks her little finger under a strand of hair that's got glued to my cheek with a tear and gently teases it off. "And you called her Rosa because you loved the pink rose that grew by our old back door. It was the only thing that wasn't grey."

I shake my head. I don't remember an old back door or any pink rose, but I know Rosa's out there somewhere, all on her own, wondering where I am, having to hide so no one sees her. I have to make Belle believe me. We have to get out of here and find Rosa.

"But she's real!"

"Of course your *shadow*'s real and I'm looking forward to meeting her when we get out of this cellar!" Belle laughs, pulling out mugs and spoons from a box under a crate. "But first I want you to meet *my* friends," she says.

She lifts the kettle off and pours the steaming water into an Aladdin lamp, stirring the leaves with an old fork.

"We don't have a teapot," she explains. "Got this from the props box." She taps the fork loudly on the side of the lamp. "Tea's up!" she calls.

There's a sound behind us and Belle's expression changes to one I haven't seen since we flew the trapeze. The one that says: *trust me.*

A huge man in a dapper tweed suit appears and sits down on the packing case next to me, neatly crossing his legs. He's entirely covered with fur; I can only just see his eyes peeping out beneath the rich crop of thicker hair growing over them, which I guess are eyebrows. His cheeks, nose, arms, hands – *everything* is covered with honey-coloured fur.

"This is Henry," Belle says. "Henry, my little sister, Tansy. She's come all the way from the Butterfly Circus. Completely by herself!"

Henry raises his fluffy eyebrows in admiration and puts out his furry hand to shake mine.

"I've heard so much about you!" he exclaims. "I feel like I know you already, you two look so alike!"

I glance at Belle and she slips me another look. It's the one I've been waiting to see for so long. It's the one that says I belong by her side.

"Missy?" Belle calls, passing Henry a mug of tea before giving me mine.

The thinnest, tallest girl I've ever seen slips out of the shadows, wearing a plain grey pinafore with a dazzling white collar. Even though the fire's blazing, she shivers as she folds herself up to sit down next to Henry and he wraps his arm round her. She snuggles against him and puts out her skinny white fingers for me to shake, but I've barely touched her before she draws her hand back, burying her face in Henry's fur.

"*Very shy*," Henry mouths as he pats Missy's arm. "Not that Pickingill cares about that!" He tuts.

"Henry was one of the first that Pickingill and Enid trapped," Belle explains.

"Enid?" I ask as I swig my tea. Its hot sweetness spreads though my body.

"The old woman – the fortune teller," Belle answers.

"I was his inspiration for the whole show! The Giant Furball, that's *me*!" Henry explains, with mock pride.

"Furball?" I ask. "Isn't that something a cat sicks up?"

Henry nods.

"He's got a huge mechanical cat upstairs. Once he's got it working properly, I'm to be…" His voice wobbles and he stops to steady himself while Missy pats his arm. After a moment, Henry straightens his back and mumbles something.

I look at Belle.

"Pickingill wanted something a bit different from a usual human cannonball and thinks it'll be funny to have Henry coughed up," she explains. "He's planned something for all of us."

"You were a human cannonball in a circus?" I ask admiringly.

Henry laughs and shakes his head. "I've never even set foot in a circus! Where I grew up, everyone's used to me so no one stares. There are no circuses on the Isle of Flora. It's all botanical gardens and horticultural displays, so I made the best of my real talents … and became a hairdresser. If there's one thing I understand, it's hair."

As if to make the point, Henry combs the fur down over his face; it is particularly glossy. He gulps his tea and wipes the droplets from the fronds of fur around his mouth, and I glance at Missy, wondering where she fits into the story.

"Missy is my washer and sweeper-upper … and dear friend. I feel just dreadful she's got mixed up in all this."

"What happened?" I ask.

"Two months ago, Pickingill strolled into my salon, bold as brass, demanding a…" he turns to Missy.

"Moustache wash and wax," Missy suggests timidly. "We had a special offer that week."

"Halfway through, he asks me to join his 'Cabinet of Curiosities'. I threw him out, then and there, his moustache only half waxed. Next day, the salon mysteriously burnt down and Missy vanished into thin air—"

"Like you, Belle!" I interrupt. She nods sadly.

"That's how Pickingill works," Henry explains, looking tenderly at Missy. "He kidnaps the person you care about most, knowing you'll follow."

"What about the mermaid?"

"That's Keziah," Belle explains.

"Who did she come to rescue?" I ask, scanning the room.

"Her horse, Apple, the one pulling Enid's wagon. Keziah adores him."

Just then there's a commotion out on the stairs that makes us all jump. The door is flung open and Enid pushes a tiny woman into the room. She falls on her back with a thud, but she's up again in a flash, banging her fists on the door. Despite her missing her fake tail and wig, I recognise her immediately: the mermaid. As she approaches, I can see her arms and neck are painted with fish scales and her face is perfectly made-up with a rosebud mouth like a china doll. She grabs a rag and begins furiously rubbing the stage make-up off her cheeks and lips, stomping across the room, cursing under her breath.

"I swear if Pickingill makes me get in that tank again—"

"Keziah!" Belle cuts in quickly. "We were just talking about you. This is Tansy."

"*You!*" Keziah gasps. "I saw you at the parade. What did you do to the elephants? Pickingill was furious!"

Belle looks at me questioningly.

"It was Rosa!" I start, but Belle just smiles, shakes her head and offers a mug to Keziah. "The mermaid trick," I say tentatively, "it hooked a lot of people in."

Keziah puts her tea down and taps her forehead. "The power of suggestion. Pickingill tells you you're about to see a miracle, so you see a miracle – a real-life mermaid. But look close and you'd see it was all smoke and mirrors. I should know – I'm in the funfair line of work myself."

"Keziah fixes carousel horses on the Isle of Jambor," Henry explains.

"*Make* them," Keziah corrects him, her flinty eyes flashing. "Make them and mend them." She crosses her arms defiantly.

"Of c–course," Henry stammers apologetically.

"Gallopers have been our bread and butter for six generations," Keziah explains. "That's how I met Pickingill." She spits his name. "Sneaked in my workshop, offering to buy one of the horses I was fixing; said it was only good for scrap. But the old rascal was really

 145

just trying to find out what he could steal to trick me into coming here." She swallows her tea and wipes her mouth on her cuff. "Anyway, whatever you did earlier, Pickingill's hopping mad and I'm sure we'll all pay for it."

I look around, shivering. "I'm sorry ... I didn't mean to make trouble for you. I just came to rescue my sister." I glance at Belle. She looks so proud of me and the joy I feel is sweeter than the hot tea.

"Well, good luck with that," Keziah says. "He keeps us all locked in here, except when he wants us onstage."

I can see what Pickingill could have in store for the rest of us. But Missy? I think of the adverts on Pickingill's caravan: *other peculiars and notables*. Missy is tall and thin, but nothing anyone would pay to see.

As if she's reading my mind, Belle says, "Missy is being trained to be a contortionist; the 'Miss Pinch' on the posters."

"Torture for a shy person to be gawped at," Henry adds.

"That's horrible," I say. "We've got to get out of here." I've been scanning the room while we've been talking. There are no windows and just the one door that Enid holds the key to. The only other escape route is high above us – a trapdoor to the stage.

"We've tried," Belle says. "I got out through the

trapdoor a few nights ago, but the monkeys are his eyes and ears. They scream the place down the second anything's wrong."

"There must be another way."

Henry shakes his head and tuts. "Pickingill always makes sure one of us is kept down here. That way we're all trapped."

Keziah nods. "We agreed we have to go together or not at all."

"All for one and one for all!" Henry chimes in heroically.

"But what if one of us could escape and raise the alarm?"

"Impossible," say Belle. "The pier is full of his cronies. Even if you managed to get out, you'd be spotted before you got very far."

All of a sudden the Butterfly Circus seems the sweetest place on earth. I think of Rosa out there in Sanctuary's streets alone. I have to find her before nightfall; she'll be terrified. I must have a look on my face because Belle reaches out and strokes my cheek.

"We'll find a way out," I tell her. "You'll see—"

But before I can say anything more, I hear the key in the lock. Enid's back.

14

Pickingill's Dream

"**R**ehearsal!" Enid barks. Henry stands and gently helps Missy to her feet, but Enid shows them the palm of her hand and they meekly sit down again. "Just you!" She points a witchy finger at me.

"Not without me!" Belle snaps, grabbing my hand and standing up. I can still hear her breath wheezing in her chest.

Enid shrugs and pushes us through the door and up the steps. Just before we reach the top, Belle whispers a quick warning in my ear.

"Pickingill is dangerous. Do as he says … for now."

Enid opens the stage door and forces us up onto the dimly lit stage. From somewhere in the auditorium I hear a snap of fingers. Suddenly, I'm in the beam of a single spotlight. A slow clap begins from the back of the auditorium, then Pickingill appears from the shadows, sauntering down the aisle between the seats.

"Finally!" he shouts. "The star of the show!"

"Don't be shy." Enid shoves me towards the front of the stage. I trip and fall.

"Careful!" Pickingill warns. "Don't bruise it." His spurs whir around as he springs up onto the stage. "I'm *so* sorry," he mumbles as he kneels down next to me and helps me to my feet.

"Don't touch her!" Belle whispers under her breath with quiet venom as she steps between him and me. I can feel her trembling as I cower behind her. Pickingill stands up and brushes the dust off his knees, before slowly circling us, looking me up and down like I'm a rare specimen. He has darting eyes and a thin, inquisitive nose, and I immediately see that he's far cleverer and more dangerous than I realised. He's not just a showman or a zookeeper – he's a hunter.

"You really are remarkable!" he purrs as he continues to circle us. "They'll come flocking to see you."

"See me *what*?"

Belle tightens her grip on my shoulder so her fingernails pinch my skin and I shut up.

"Just *you*! You won't need to *do* anything. Just be *yourself*." My spine turns cold as he talks. "You're like alabaster. *La crème de la crème*!" He pauses. "Of course, the specs will have to go ... good work, Enid."

He pulls out a snakeskin wallet from his jacket. Enid eyes it hungrily but as he rifles through it, her expression changes to weary acceptance.

"Put it on the tab," he says, smiling insincerely.

Enid scowls and stomps off across the stage. She flicks a switch at the side and suddenly, the main lights come on, flooding the theatre with a yellowish glow. Pickingill opens his arms wide in wonder.

"It needs a lick of paint, but this will be the arena to showcase the pinnacle of my life's work!"

We're standing on a huge semi-circular stage with two archways at either side, half hidden by scaffolding encrusted with pigeon droppings. I look out over the auditorium; three aisles cut through seats covered with torn and faded red velvet. Daylight streams through holes in the roof, lighting the top tiers, encircled by balconies with cherubs gilded with patches of gold leaf that's mostly been washed away in the rain. Fancy gold mirrors are hung on the walls and over it all, a dusty candelabra drips with a crop of crystal drops, the colour of hail.

I squint up into the spotlight rigging to see if I can spot Rosa, hoping against hope she found a way to follow, but all I find lurking in the shadows are the silhouettes of the rest of Pickingill's monkeys. They are everywhere; squatting on the edge of the balconies and rickety towers of scaffolding, their yellow eyes shining. There must be at least a hundred of them, a colony of different breeds; not just capuchins, but spider monkeys with long, spindly arms, golden tamarins crested with bright orange fur and howler monkeys, famous for their booming cries. Now and then a peanut shell skitters to the floor, but otherwise they're all soundless, as if waiting for something.

On one side of the stage is an orchestral platform with stands for music and a drum kit that's seen better days. On the other, leaning against the wall, are warped plywood backdrops: a haunted house, a flowery garden scene and some trees. But taking up most of the stage is an enormous automaton of a cat, its ears brushing the spotlights. It's clothed in strips of what looks like real fur and I shudder to think how many cats were skinned to make it. The fur is so badly sewn together the stitches look like scars and its mouth hangs limply open. A spring juts through its neck where the fur is singed black.

Pickingill twirls back to look at me. I feel like a mouse caught in the sightline of a hawk. "I did this all for *you*!"

I open my mouth to speak, but Belle gives my hand a sharp squeeze and I clamp my lips shut.

"The two of you ... but *especially* you," he says, continuing to gaze at me, "will help make my shows great again. You will bring it much-needed *cachet*. Here you can *shine*, like the star you truly are!"

He sashays over to where two ropes are coiled around an iron cleat hook and begins unwinding them, still talking in his soft, menacing voice.

"I'm so pleased that you're finally here. I was always struck by your unique colour. Or lack of it." He smirks. "Sadly your parents didn't see your potential..."

I shoot Belle a questioning look, but she just looks away sadly. She doesn't have the answers.

"Our parents?" I ask in disbelief. "Where are they? Did you do something to them?"

Pickingill rolls his eyes. "I didn't *do* anything to them, except offer them the opportunity of a lifetime – the chance to see their child perform in the greatest show in Gala."

He finishes unhooking the ropes and gently tugs them. A crumpled curtain slowly shunts across the back of the stage and there's a sudden dank smell as green mould spores speckle the air.

"Unfortunately, they decided to take you on a little boat trip. All very hush-hush. Do you have *any* idea how much time I lost tracking you down? And when I did, Fratellini was as unhelpful as *they'd* been! He wouldn't even let me *meet* you, so I was *forced* to find other ways to make your acquaintance." He tugs the ropes again. "You'd think a tiger on the loose would frighten two little girls out of their caravan. I mean, how old were you then?" Pickingill asks silkily.

Belle and I share a look. He's talking about my nightmare. I was seven, she was nine. She'd been reading me a bedtime story when we heard screams. The tiger had escaped. Belle told me to count the flowers on the quilt, bolted the door, then grabbed the stick she uses to scare snakes when we go into the forest. This is the moment I always wake up sobbing or sweating, begging Belle to stay with me.

I struggle to remember what happened next. I have to tease the memory out, like it's a thread I'm separating from a tangle of others. Here it comes: the tiger's snarl as it catches our scent, its claws scraping the wagon door. Then, out of the blue, a forget-me-not blue, I recall the Belle I forgot too; standing in her dressing gown, brandishing the stick like a sword, fierce as a warrior queen. But I see something else too; her cheeks are *wet*. She's so scared, she's crying with fear, yet she was still ready to fight a tiger for me. Not in all those death-defying trapeze stunts have I ever seen anyone be braver. In my jumble of unwanted memories I have discovered a jewel; a lost memory of my sister. How could I have forgotten that? How could I have let envy and lies creep between us, like ivy between brickwork? I feel a second flush of shame.

"I'll admit you come into your own in an emergency, that's for sure."

"*You* let the tiger out?" Belle murmurs in disbelief, speaking to him for the first time. "Our fortune teller died!"

"The tiger *killed* her?!" I gasp.

Pickingill shrugs nonchalantly and tugs the ropes harder. The curtain shunts an inch and there's an angry squeaking from somewhere high up. The monkeys become rigid-backed with interest.

"So the fire ... that was you too?" Belle blinks in disbelief.

"*Mea culpa* – I am to blame." Pickingill lays the flat of his hand on his chest and bows.

"We could have been killed too," I whisper.

"*Au contraire,* dear heart," he says, ducking as a bat swoops over his head. "I've *always* been there to save you; ready with a bucket to put out the fire, pistol cocked to shoot the tiger." He fondles the top of his ivory cane. "I've had plenty of practice on safari."

I realise the cane has been carved from an elephant's tusk and another wave of fury washes over me, but before I can say anything I hear a squeak and glance up. One of the spider monkeys gazes down at me, chewing something that looks like a bit of umbrella sticking out of its mouth – the unlucky bat's wing.

"Anyway, fascinating as this *tête-à-tête* is," Pickingill trills, yanking the curtain rope once more, "we have a show to put on. And you are the star of it! Admit it. You miss it, don't you? Being in the spotlight? The applause? I mean, you must be fed up with being in your sister's shadow?"

I glance at Belle and the smile in her eyes tells me she's got my back. I smile too; nothing and *no one* will ever come between us again.

Pickingill sidles back to the edge of the stage to a line of levers for the stagehands to control special effects. He picks up an old oil can with a long nozzle like an anteater and begins oiling each cog.

"Obviously we need some kind of story to sell your

act. Something like…" He scrunches up his face in concentration as if an idea has just struck him. "A trapeze! I'd been thinking an ordinary ghost, but we can bring *your* personal struggle into it. Yes, I can see it already!"

He rubs his hands together with glee and runs over to the drum kit. He discards his cane, then starts beating the drums loudly.

"I'll call it the Flying Ghost!" he shouts. "You're the star of the show … flying through the sky, but you become arrogant and attempt a foolish trick and … you fall from the trapeze…" Pickingill starts a loud drum roll, his eyes glittering. "And … die!" He smashes the cymbal so hard it bounces off its stand. "But you loved the trapeze so much you return to … *haunt* it. Ta-dah!" After a last drum roll he takes a low, graceful bow. "What do you think?"

What do I think? I think I was the best trapezist anyone ever saw. I was strong and free. I worked hard to be the stuff of dreams and just because I can't fly any more doesn't mean I'm going to be part of Pickingill's nightmare.

"*It*." I say quietly.

"Say what?" Pickingill asks breathlessly.

"You called me 'it'," I say. "When Enid pushed me,

you said, 'Don't bruise *it*.' You don't even see me as human. You're a *monster*."

"Nonsense … I'm an artist!"

He blows the little silver whistle around his neck. Immediately four tamarin monkeys scamper across the balcony edges and scuttle onto the rigging above the stage. They slowly winch down the backdrop. As it creaks into view, Belle gasps. It's a garishly painted circus scene, clearly meant to be the Butterfly Circus. Pickingill has even painted members of our own troupe: there's Doris and Boris waiting in the wings and a figure meant to be Mrs Fratellini sits on the banquette. Across the top is a banner decorated with dozens of butterflies fluttering prettily around the words:

Pickingill's Cabinet of Curiosities

Pickingill clasps his hands and sighs with pleasure, then scans the room for Enid. She's slumped in a front-row seat, munching her way through a bag of peanuts.

"Bring Furball and Pinch up," he orders.

Enid sighs and pockets the peanuts, then trudges off down to the trap room.

"Time to get this show on the road!" He smirks.

15

Dress Rehearsals

A single brilliant spotlight shimmers on the cat automaton, now centre stage, while two tamarin monkeys creep along the edge of the footlights, lighting the candles. Missy is already in costume: a full-length leotard patterned like a snake, so tight she can hardly move. Her act is to be trapped by Pickingill, playing the Great Safari Hunter, who then squeezes her into a bell jar and winches her across the audience. They can take turns spinning and knocking the jar like a *piñata*. In the darkness of the auditorium, I can hear Pickingill's sausage dog barking.

I squint into the rafters again, wondering if Rosa could have found her way inside to help us escape. But there are just more monkeys, chattering and shrieking as they rig up the bell jar above the stage. There's a creak from the door to the trap room stairs and Enid thrusts Henry towards us.

"Ready, Furball?" Pickingill shouts, banging the cat's side, making it tremble and rock precariously. There's an ugly metal clatter from inside as something breaks off and falls. "Safe as houses!" He laughs. "But I got you this anyway." He rummages in a wooden tea chest with HELF & SAFETY chalked on the side and pulls out an old colander with string tied from the handles.

"It's too dangerous," I whisper to Belle as Henry gingerly adjusts the colander on his head. He shrugs helplessly and ties the strings under his chin. Pickingill has kept Keziah down in the trap room so Henry doesn't dare disobey orders.

As Pickingill opens a small door in the side of the cat, I glimpse two tyres with hooks holding them back tight against two thick bands of rubber, like a giant catapult. Henry wriggles in with a grunt and lies face down on the tyres. Pickingill slams the door shut, causing a sprinkle of red rust to rain down. He slowly cranks a creaky handle to wind the mechanism up until there's a loud *click*, then he pirouettes over to a lever sticking out of the cat's leg and rubs his hands together. The sausage dog scampers up onto one of the seats, its fur bristling, barking even louder.

"We have to stop this!" I say to Belle, but as I step forward she puts her hand out to hold me back.

"Ready in there?" Pickingill trills, his fingers playing on the lever.

"He needs a safety net!" I blurt out. There's nothing like falling from a trapeze to make you appreciate a net.

"Ah yes!" Pickingill giggles. "I nearly forgot!" He makes a signal and four of the monkeys scamper up each side of the huge arch over the stage holding the ends of a raggedy net between them. There are massive holes in it.

"That's going to be useless!" Belle whispers fearfully, but Pickingill has already banged the lever down. Missy grabs Belle's hand, her eyes widening in dismay. The cat shudders and stretches its neck, its head wobbling dangerously. A loud clatter comes from deep within its body and steel claws slide out from its toes like knives. It starts heaving, then rocking back and forth, until eventually the jaws creak apart. Pickingill dances a little jig of anticipation. The cat's eyelids flicker open and two bright beams of light shine out. Suddenly there's a grinding sound, followed by a puff of smoke from one of the ears. There's a bang and a firework shoots out of the other ear, spitting across the rafters and startling the monkeys from their perches. Missy screams and the dog barks louder than ever, yapping so hard it actually bounces backwards with the strain of it.

"Someone shut Snipe up!" Pickingill yells. More smoke belches out from the cat's seams. There's a polite cough from inside.

"Sorry to interrupt," Henry calls out courteously, "but I think I might be on fire."

I rush towards the door with Belle close behind me, but instantly the monkeys leap down through the rigging, their sharp teeth bared, blocking our way.

"Good job!" Enid chimes in casually, rolling her eyes behind Pickingill's back as she tosses a peanut in her mouth. "You need to get that Keziah up there. She's so diddy, she could get right inside the workings. And she knows what she's doing."

"*I* know what I'm doing!" Pickingill yells, yanking the door open. Henry tumbles out and the smell of singed fur and smoke billows out across the stage. "You're just *too* fat!" Pickingill barks, dragging Henry to his feet and shaking him. "Look at the state of you!"

Henry's fur is covered in black soot and a small flame is still licking the side of his neck. One of the monkeys scuttles up holding a pail of water and throws it over both of Pickingill and Henry.

"Idiot!" Pickingill snarls, swiping at the monkey as it dodges out of the way. He grabs Henry by the collar and pushes him towards Missy.

"Get him cleaned up," he orders. "Then get back up here!" For several seconds he gazes at the smoking wreck of his automaton, clasping his head in his hands, then he turns and makes a low, gracious bow to Belle and me. "Forgive me ... I'm surrounded by amateurs," he says ingratiatingly.

"The only amateur around here is you!" I mutter under my breath. Belle shoots me a warning look.

"This act needs a little work," Pickingill continues, frowning at the ash raining down over the stage. "However, you two ladies are consummate professionals and I'm sure you've performed many dangerous stunts in your time." He leers at Belle as the monkeys lower a rickety trapeze towards her. Its ropes are frayed and the bar is made of splintered bamboo. "Time to show us what you're made of," he says and pushes Belle over to the trapeze.

"That's not safe," I say. Pickingill purses his lips together.

"I'll be all right," Belle says, but I can hear her breath

rattling in her chest. She gives me her brightest smile and quickly climbs up, taking a tentative swing back and forth. The bamboo creaks loudly.

Pickingill squints down his long nose. "You'll make a wonderful butterfly, Belle, especially when Bullseye has finished designing your … outfit."

The monkey lowers a second swing that looks even more precarious than the first and pushes it towards me.

"Why isn't this one in costume?" Pickingill snaps. "And I said no specs!"

Enid unhooks a hanger from a rack and plods over, handing Pickingill something that looks like a pair of old net curtains. Pickingill thrusts them into my arms.

"Quickly!" he shouts. "We haven't got all day!"

This past week must have changed me; Rosa has changed me. She might not be here, but she's in my soul. Her beetle-black has rubbed off on me, just enough to remind me that I should be free; just enough to make me feel brave enough to refuse to do as I'm told. My mysterious, sticky-fingered, stubborn shadow wouldn't let herself be ordered around and nor will I.

"Hurry up!" Pickingill snaps.

I let the bundle of clothes fall to the floor.

"No."

"Tansy!" Belle whispers desperately, but even she can't stop me.

"No," I say again, but louder.

Pickingill glares furiously at me. "Have it your way," he says sinisterly. "Your sister can test it." Pickingill grabs Belle's wrist and yanks her off her trapeze and over to mine.

It all happens so quickly. One second there's a broom leaning against the cat automaton and the next it's in my hands and I've jumped in front them. I'm trembling with rage and sweat's prickling my back.

It's my turn to be the warrior queen. I'm ready to take down the tiger.

"Don't. You. Touch. My. Sister." My voice doesn't even sound human. It comes from somewhere deeper and darker, somewhere where my anger burns white-hot.

Pickingill just laughs at me.

I leap at him, jabbing him hard in the ribs with the broom. He yelps and bends double, but I come at him again. This time he's ready and grabs the other end of the broom and tries to wrench it from my hands. But I won't let go.

"You little brute!" he snarls, pushing me backwards.

I try to stand my ground but he's too strong. He

pushes me again and I stumble to the floor. Above my head I hear a gasp of fury as Belle springs forward, followed by a cry of pain from Pickingill. I look up to see Pickingill clutching a deep scratch down the side of his face where Belle has clawed him.

"Take her to Bullseye!" he yells at Enid.

I scramble to my feet, but before I can reach Belle, Pickingill blows his whistle and a gang of monkeys drop from above like a battalion of hairy, shrieking soldiers. They encircle me, their breath sickly sweet with the pear-drop smell of rotten banana.

I hear a scream and for a second I can't work out if it's mine or Belle's before realising our two screams have woven together. I fight my way across the stage as she's dragged into the auditorium. The monkeys scratch and snap at me but all I can think about, all I care about is Belle. I drop down to the sticky carpet between the seats and my hand falls on the bag of peanuts Enid has been chomping. I grab it and swing it wildly, like a slingshot, out across the seats. As it twirls over the auditorium, peanuts skitter everywhere and the monkeys scatter. I stagger to my feet in time to see Enid and Belle disappear through a pair of heavy swing doors at the back. I grab my chance and race up the aisle after them.

"Snipe!" Pickingill shrieks. The little dog hurls himself over the seats, tearing towards me as fast as his stumpy legs will let him, his steel teeth snapping like scissors. When he gets to the end of the row, he launches himself into the air. I'm too slow to duck and he crashes into me, knocking me down to the ground. By the time I've got to my feet again and pushed Snipe off, the theatre doors have snapped shut.

I've lost Belle all over again.

16

Cloud Swings

"**Y**ou can cool down in here!" Pickingill snarls, sending me sprawling back into the trap room. "Should have guessed sisters would be trouble!" He slams the door in my face. The key turns in the lock. I can't stop myself from bursting into tears. Keziah rushes over.

"What happened?" she asks, her face ashen. Henry is close behind her; his fur is burnt to a frizz on one side of his face and black streaks of wet soot have run down his chest.

"They took Belle!" I sob.

"Where?"

I try to answer but can't catch my breath through the crying. After a few seconds, Keziah loses patience and pokes me. She might look as fragile as a doll, but her finger's sharper than Spinnet's.

"Get a grip!" she snaps. "Where did they take her?"

"He said … to Bullseye's?"

"Oh dear!" Henry mumbles, shuffling from foot to foot. "Oh dear, oh dear."

"What does that mean?" I shout.

"Pickingill said she'd be perfect as a…" His voice trails off.

"Butterfly," Keziah finishes. "Rumour is, anyone that's not…" Her mouth makes a funny shape while she tries to find the right word. "Anyone not *different* enough to be an exhibit is taken to Bullseye's. To be … changed."

I get it now; I remember the man standing on the pier next to a tattoo parlour. I remember the pictures: the crocodile-woman and the eagle-man. Belle is going to be a real butterfly in a fake Butterfly Circus.

They're going to tattoo her.

I go cold. If he dares touch a hair on her head! I feel sick just thinking about it. I have to get out of here. I have to find her again. I push past Keziah towards the trapdoor in the ceiling. That's the only way out. Missy shakes her head as she watches me.

"It's always locked," she whispers.

Keziah nods. "We're on a pier. Even if you screamed for help, no one would ever hear you over the sound of the sea."

Suddenly it hits me. Keziah has given me the answer: we're on a *pier*. I can't go up ... but I can go down. I begin to pace around the room.

"What are you doing, dear?" Henry asks, but I hold my hand up for silence.

For the first few steps I hear nothing but waves, then finally one loud *creak* sounds beneath my foot. The noise I was listening for – a loose board. I grab the fork from the Aladdin lamp and drop to my knees.

"What is it?" Henry asks, leaning over me as I lever the fork between the gap in the boards. The nails start to squeak as I prise the board up.

"You can't get out that way..." Henry looks at Keziah for help.

I ignore him and curl my fingers under the edge of the board, puffing and panting as I try to heave it up, but I'm not strong enough. Just then Henry nudges me out of the way; there's the sound of splintering wood as he twists it to one side. I kneel next to the hole, looking through.

My stomach flips in fear. Far below, the sea is the colour of blackcurrant cordial, streaked orange from the setting sun. The waves smash into the jagged grey rocks, which were scattered by the volcanic eruption these islands are formed from. Every fibre in my body tells me to lay the board back down again, but I force myself to sit down on the edge of the hole.

"You're crazy!" Keziah whispers in awe, but I have to do *something*, even if it is the *crazy* thing.

"If Pickingill comes for me, pretend I'm sick. Once I've got Belle, we'll come back for you."

"All for one," Henry says bravely.

"And one for all," I finish, forcing a smile.

I lower myself through the gap. My heart batters the inside of my ribs, like it doesn't want to come with me, and I feel for the first iron girder with the tips of my toes. It's no wider than my foot.

"Good luck!" Henry lowers the board over my head. For one horrible moment I imagine slipping and being washed out to sea, but I push the image out of my mind.

Here and there, sunlight spikes the stagnant dark, revealing gulls perching on slimy corners. The pier is built on huge pairs of iron columns linked by girders, supported by lacework arches. If I can crawl through the lattice of iron, I might be able to pull myself up onto the pier by the tattoo shop without ever being seen.

Fear has numbed all feeling in my feet, so I tap my foot in front of me to get a sense of balance. I take a first tentative step when a gull unexpectedly flutters up in an explosion of feathers and I jump in shock, nearly falling. The Glowbell slips out from my cloak and dangles precariously on its chain. I just manage to keep my grip, but now I can't unclench my fingers from the strut they've gripped. I'm frozen with fear and no amount of willpower can change that.

"I'm stuck!" I whisper.

"Me too," comes a voice from ahead. I can hardly believe it. There's a dark shadow behind the next girder.

"Rosa!" I shout.

As she peeps around at me, I notice her eyes are shimmery and wide, and I realise she's been crying too.

"I tried to follow you, but I couldn't get past that horrible dog, growling and snapping at me. He chased me around that theatre and he actually *tore* me..." She stops gabbling long enough to hold out her leg for me to see a small hole in it. "So I tried to come this way, but I didn't realise it'd be so—"

A huge wave suddenly splashes against the pier and icy water sprays over us. The roosting gulls squawk and scream. Rosa squeaks and disappears behind the pillar again. "It's so *dark* down here," she says, her voice trembling.

She needs my help. I grab the next girder, dragging myself forwards an inch.

"Take my Glowbell," I tell her. "If you shake it, even if you just move, it gives off quite a lot of light. Especially this one."

With my free hand, I stretch out the gold chain. In that moment, one of the last needles of sunlight pricks the gloom and the shadow of Belle's Glowbell lands on the girder just above Rosa's head.

She beams. "*Oooh*! That's pretty; a slice of rainbow."

Instead of taking the Glowbell dangling from my hand, she reaches up and lifts its *shadow* down and hooks it over her head. Against her, it instantly disappears from view but she must be shaking it, because I can see teardrops of light sprinkling out across where her heart would be, just a little fainter than the real Glowbell.

"How did you do that?" I gasp, putting the Glowbell back around my neck.

"Do what?" she says casually as she climbs over to me, no longer afraid now she has some light. "Did you find Belle?"

"Yes, but now I've lost her again. I need to get back

up to the pier without being seen," I say, looking around.

"There's a walkway, over there." She shakes her Glowbell shadow so that hundreds of tiny jewelled lights burst out, in kaleidoscope spray, illuminating a rickety iron walkway on the other side of the pier. But there's no way across to it that I can see.

"It's impossible," I whisper, looking down at the surf pounding the rocks below.

"You can fly..." She smiles.

"I'm not a bird!" I laugh.

"No! Like you used to ... on the trapeze."

I stop smiling. She can't be serious. I can't ever fly the trapeze again, just thinking about it brings me out in a cold sweat.

"I think I can *crawl*," I say, looking at the treacherously oily girders ahead.

Rosa shakes her head. "You'll slip and fall," she tells me bluntly. "And I'll never find you again ... not down there." She peers at the dark, frothing sea below.

I've never heard her sound this solemn. She sounds older; older than everything.

"I can't do it."

"You can," Rosa says. "I won't let you fall. I caught you before, didn't I?"

I look down at the rocks and suddenly remember my fall; the terrifying rush of air, the certainty I was going to die, then feeling something damp and silky against my hand. Everyone always said that I must have grabbed the silks to break my fall because of the enormous rip in them, the rip that Mrs Fratellini put on display; the miracle. Now I realise they saw what they expected to see, not the truth. In a sudden flash I remember clearly now; I didn't catch hold of the silks – Rosa caught hold of me.

"You saved me," I gasp.

Rosa nods. "So trust me now."

"But we don't have a trapeze. Or even a rope."

Rosa slithers up the iron strut and hangs onto the girder above my head. As I watch, she starts stretching her arms out, longer and longer. At the same time, she pushes out her legs until they're three times as long, then she hooks her feet up and over the girder too. Her body starts to droop and lengthen, like when you pinch bubble gum and pull it out from your mouth. She sways in the gloom, slowly becoming a long, thick piece of rope. She's turned herself into a cloud swing.

"How do you do that?" I say admiringly.

"One of my many talents." Rosa smiles. "I'm very good at stretching."

I steady myself and take deep breaths. Rosa starts swinging gently back and forth, building momentum until I can almost touch her. I squint ahead at the iron walkway, sensing its distance with every fibre in my body. I'm not sure I can do this. It might only be five seconds in the air, but that's a long time to be terrified.

"Ready?" she asks, still swinging in the breeze.

I smell the faintest scent of pine mixed into the briny tang from the sea. I put my arms out either side, raising them to shoulder level and take a deep breath, trying to calm myself.

"Come on!" Rosa laughs. "I can't hang around here all day!"

It's the third time she's swung close enough for me to grab her. As she drops away into the dark canyon between us, she disappears and only her flickering Glowbell shadow shows me where she is. From the blackness I hear her whisper, "I won't let you fall."

She's flying back towards me again.

Now or never.

I straighten my back, bring my arms together and flex my fingers out. I bend my knees and put my chin up.

"Trust me and jump," she whispers.

Timing is everything.

I leap into my fear; the pure, drenching fear that's been cramping my arms and legs every time I've tried to climb. The fear that took away my passion, the fear that made me lie to my sister. Only the hot bolt of terror in my throat stops me screaming.

Then suddenly I'm clenching Rosa tight between my fists, plunging towards the waves. My feet point downwards as I jump, and I drop with sickening speed towards the sea and rocks below. I'm in the dark; falling, but not alone.

It only takes one beat of my heart to meet the lowest point of Rosa's swing. It's like a punch, where the tug between my weight and her strength suddenly bites. The instant I feel it, I flip my legs forwards and lift my body up towards the walkway, raising Rosa too with my power. But just as I'm about to let go, Rosa whispers in my ear, "Not yet!" and at the last second I tighten my grip on her. We plummet backwards into the darkness again.

On the second swing, I fling my legs behind me to capture every ounce of energy I have. My feet are so high above my head I'm tiptoeing on the underside of the pier like an upside-down ballerina in an upside-down world, with the sea for my sky and the surf for my clouds. Our two Glowbells merge and refract; light and shadows speckling the dank and rusty girders. I feel my muscles spasm but somehow Rosa is holding on to me as much as I'm holding on to her and I know I won't fall. Then we drop again, faster and faster in a swoop that leaves my stomach behind.

This time there's no tug of war between weight and will, no tension between my body and Rosa's spirit. We are flying together and as my body soars, it takes my heart with it. My feet touch the walkway and I feel Rosa deliver me, as carefully as putting a fallen fledging back in its nest. I grab an iron rail with one hand and then pull Rosa up next to me. In the blink of an eye she shrinks back to her rightful shape.

"You did it!" she says breathlessly, her eyes star-bright.

"*We* did it!" I laugh, hugging her tightly.

17

Bullseye

Halfway down the pier, we find a small metal ladder that leads to a low gate in the railings, with MAINTENANCE engraved on a brass plaque. We push it open and step through. The sun has slid back behind the mountain peaks and the twilight is scented with roast turmeric and cumin, wafting over from the shore. The pier is closing up for the night and only a few lanterns are still alight on their posts, twinkling and dancing on the sea breeze.

We race to Bullseye's tattoo parlour, but he's nowhere to be seen and the kiosk is deserted and shuttered up. We try the door but it's bolted shut.

"We're closed!" bellows a voice. "Come back tomorrow!"

"Let's check the windows," I whisper.

Rosa goes left and I go right, checking the building until we meet by the last window; the only one not shuttered up. It's an old sash window, half sagging on its ropes with a tiny gap at the top. Taking care not to be seen, we slowly peep up over the peeling windowsill.

The first thing I clap eyes on is Bullseye's bullseye, red as a gobstopper, bang in the centre of his shiny bald head with four rings alternating red and black around it. He's hunched over his counter, organising his tattooing instruments under the lamplight, screwing a needle onto the tattoo machine. The second thing I notice is the skull tattoo on the side of his neck, with a snake wriggling through the eye sockets. On the other side, the word "Mummy" is surrounded with red roses.

The rest of the room is lined with shelves of hundreds of ink bottles, sparkling with different-coloured tints, all meticulously arranged according to their various hues. Behind Bullseye I spot Belle. She's got her back to us and has been strapped into a leather chair on wheels. Crouching on the ground, I can just see the top of Enid's head.

"Stop wriggling, you little brat," she snaps as she tightens the strap around Belle's ankles.

I feel sick seeing Belle so helpless. Our whole lives, Belle has been the strong one, the one who did the looking after; a proper big sister.

"How long's she going to take, Bull?" Enid asks as she plonks herself down on a stool and thumbs through a huge book.

"Maybe half tonight, take a break, finish tomorrow," Bullseye replies.

Anger prickles my skin like nettle rash.

"What are they doing to her?" Rosa says quietly.

"How about this one?" Enid asks, holding up the book for him to see. Bullseye looks up, rolling his eyes like a sulky teenager and we duck out of sight again. I just have time to see a picture of butterfly wings, with filigree edges and hearts in their centres.

"I told you, Mummy – Pickingill wants her *really* bright!" he mutters.

I peek in again just in time to see him give a thumbs-up to an even more garish picture of butterfly wings. They are full of fierce turquoises, stinging greens and citrus yellows.

"We've got to get her out, right now," I whisper to Rosa.

Bullseye slides a small trolley over to Belle, which rattles with bottles of ink as he drags it. He ties an apron on, pulls a pair of glasses from his pocket and slots them over his nose. Then he swivels Belle's chair around and rolls up her sleeve, exposing her bare arm. I hear a low humming start up, like an angry hornet. Bullseye has turned on his machine.

"Leave it to me," Rosa answers, her chin jutting out angrily. Before I can blink, she slides through the gap at the top of the window. I watch her glide through the shadows of the bottles and boxes of needles strewn over the counter. The bottles of inks rattle, but neither Enid nor Bullseye seem to notice over the sound of the machine.

"She's going to look a treat," Bullseye says, grinning wolfishly as he lowers the needle towards Belle's arm. "Head to toe."

What if Rosa can't stop him? I look around desperately for something to break the glass, but find nothing. I turn back just in time to see a single bottle fly off the shelf and spin across the room. Trails of blood-red ink swirl behind it and splat down on Bullseye's head.

He yelps in shock and drops his tattoo machine. He puts one hand on his head and looks at his palm, then at the ceiling, then back at his hand. Slowly, he swivels around on his chair and gapes stupidly at the shelves. Rosa suddenly swishes her legs out, sending dozens of

181

bottles whirling up into the air, all popping open simul-taneously. Ultra-marine, indigo, cobalt, emerald, jade and teal inks rain down. They splash over Bullseye's head, running into his eyes. While he's blinded, Rosa grabs a fistful of Enid's hair and yanks it.

"Ow!" she screams. "A ghost!"

Enid rushes for the door but trips over and falls. Bullseye blindly bangs his hand on the trolley, smash-ing more bottles as he searches for something to mop his eyes. Rosa quickly slithers over to Belle and tugs her straps loose, then hops back into the shadows again. I can see her crescent-shaped eyes sparkling with mischief as she watches the pandemonium; she's having the time of her life.

Enid's still screaming as she gets to her feet and wrenches the door open, racing out without a back-wards glance. Belle wriggles her feet free and kicks out, sending Bullseye's chair rocketing across the room, spinning on its wheels. As he twirls past, he manages to rub some of the ink off with his cuffs and for a second we lock eyes. I smile my slowest, creepiest smile and Bullseye lets out a blood-curdling scream.

"It's a g–ghost!" he squeals, pointing right at me. Another bottle of ink suddenly smashes on his head and he squeals.

At the sound of Bullseye's scream, Belle looks up and sees me too. I race round to the front door and run in. Her face lights up with a mixture of delight and shock, but I put my finger to my lips. Bullseye is still crashing around blindly, looking for something to rinse his eyes. Together we shove the chair under him, knocking him off balance. He topples into it and Belle quickly buckles the leather straps. I suddenly spot something glinting on the floor. Enid's dropped the trap-room key and I snatch it up, then Belle and I roll Bullseye's chair out of the door and onto the pier. Once we've picked up enough speed, on Belle's nod, we let go and Bullseye sails off down the pier, whimpering, "Mummy! Mummy!" Just then, there's a squawking overhead as a gull swoops across the pier and deposits a large white splat of poop on his bullseye tattoo. I smile.

"Let's go and get the others out," Belle says as she turns to run back towards the theatre.

I hear panting and realise it's Rosa, hovering in the doorway to Bullseye's shop, her eyes glittering with excitement.

"C'mon!" I shout and she runs after me, streams of ink trailing behind her like water off a duck's back.

"How did you do that?" Belle asks breathlessly when I catch up.

"I didn't – Rosa did!" I tell her, jerking my thumb behind where Rosa is skipping along happily. Belle half frowns for a second before laughing at me. Rosa was right: people see what they expect to see, not what's really there.

We all race on towards the theatre. It seems to be floating on the end of the pier as evening mists slither and coil around it. It's deathly quiet as we creep up to the large blue gates I passed through before. But this time, they're locked.

"How are we going to get in?" Belle whispers.

"The animal pens," I whisper back.

"Then what? We can't get into the trap room!"

"Yes we can," I say triumphantly, holding up the key.

We creep through the mist, hand in hand, to a semi-circle of squat animal pens around the back. Luckily the pen doors have been so loosely chained that there's a wide enough gap for Belle and me to squeeze through. Inside the two elephants that pulled Pickingill's carriages are huddling close, their trunks coiled together for comfort. The younger one has been crying and tears have carved dark tracks down her dusty trunk. On her flank I can see fresh whip marks. The pen is bare and there's no window.

"*Ça va?*" I whisper as I scratch their foreheads. They

sniff at my hair and seem to know they should keep quiet, barely making a sound as Belle and I tiptoe past. I see they're shackled by manacles on their back legs, tethered to an iron ring in the floor. I drop to my knees to try to open them but they're locked. At the same moment, both elephants lift their trunks in a sort of salute. I look behind to see Rosa slide in from outside.

"You free your friends," she whispers, "while I free mine."

I hesitate. I hate the thought of leaving her again.

"Go…" she says. "I'll be fine."

I run to catch up with Belle and we push open the door into a gloomy corridor, lit only by red EXIT lights. This must be where large props, like the giant cat are wheeled in, but now it's a museum of Pickingill's vanity. One wall is covered by photos of him wearing a safari helmet, his rifle at a jaunty angle, his foot on the head of a tusk-less elephant. Alongside the photos are the glass-eyed heads of his other kills: two black rhinos, a dozen gazelles, and four zebras. On the opposite wall are intricate technical drawings of the cat automaton and other blueprints for mechanicals; giant versions of the ones we saw in the old playhouse, each one to feature a human element. The Giant Furball act was just the start. We reach the end of the corridor and creep through an archway onto the stage, emerging right by the giant cat.

I look up warily, but all the monkeys are asleep on the rafters, hunched like hairy gargoyles against the moonlight spilling through the roof. We hurry across the stage and down the stairway to the trap room where we quickly unlock the door. There's a scuffling from the corner as Henry stumbles to his feet. He blinks blearily in confusion.

"You came back!" he whispers. "You really came back!"

We wake Keziah and Missy, and exchange quick hugs.

"How do we get out?" Keziah asks worriedly as we head back up to the stage.

"Through there," I tell them quietly, pointing to the corridor we came up. "Not a sound!"

"But I've got to get Apple!" Keziah whispers frantically, "I can't leave him … I'll catch you up!" Before anyone can stop her, she flits through a second archway that must lead to the stables. I put my finger to my lips and beckon the others to follow me instead.

The moon is even brighter now. As we creep across the stage, I see that the monkeys are clustered together in shivering heaps around the scaffolding, huddling for warmth against the chilly drafts whistling through the roof. We're walking in single file, like elephants, silently padding across the floor when something brittle crunches under my foot. A dropped nut.

We freeze, holding our breath. One heartbeat, two heartbeats. There's a murmur from above; a scuffle. The silhouette of a tamarin monkey scampers across a rafter, then shrieks.

"Run!" I yell.

18

Revenge

The nests of monkeys burst apart as they wake up, screaming and wailing to raise the alarm. We hurtle across the stage towards the archway that leads to the animals' pens and I skid to a stop. Pickingill is heading up the corridor towards us. Snipe races on ahead, immediately snapping at my ankles and barking furiously.

"Going somewhere?" Pickingill sneers, sending a shiver down my spine. He's wearing a monogrammed dressing gown, embroidered with his initials: H.P. As he casually ties the silky cord, he tuts and shakes his head, then thrusts down a lever sticking out of the wall. The whole stage floods with light.

"You too, Keziah?" he calls, pulling his cane from

where it's tucked under his armpit and waving it disdainfully.

I shoot a look over my shoulder and see Keziah coming towards us. She's managed to rescue Apple, but now a gang of monkeys are slowly stalking their way down from the rafters and across the balconies towards them.

Pickingill gazes at us slowly, one by one, a look of disappointment in his eyes, as if we're all naughty children. "Nice of you to join us again, Belle, although it seems you've skipped out on Bullseye. How clever of you ... and your *sister*." He reaches out and grabs my shoulder. "Looks like you'll be needing exclusive accommodation from now on."

"We're leaving." I look at the others for support. No one speaks.

"Is this your idea, Miss Pinch?" Pickingill asks Missy, tightening his dressing gown cord. Typical bully – go for the most afraid.

"It was my—" I start to say, but Missy interrupts me.

"It was all of us." She sounds calm, but she's trembling as she speaks.

"That's right. W–we'd all like to go home," Henry stammers nervously. "P–please."

"W–w–w–would you?" Pickingill mimics. "And

all this time I thought you wanted to be something special, Furball!"

"Leave him alone!" Belle hisses, shoving him in the chest. Pickingill jolts back, making his spurs spin. He draws a sharp, angry breath, then blows his whistle. Snipe barks excitedly.

Immediately there's a scurrying as a group of capuchins encircle us. They grab Henry, who's nearest, and drag him back towards the trap room. Missy tries to pull him out of their grasp as Snipe races around her, snapping at her ankles. Another five monkeys charge at Keziah and Apple, but in a flash, Keziah's up on Apple's back, holding on as he rears up, snorting and stamping his hooves on the ground. The monkeys scatter, but some of the boldest spring up to wrestle Keziah down.

Belle and I race around the side of the cat and take cover. There's a loud jangle of cymbals and when I peep out, I see Henry ripping up Pickingill's drum kit and batting away the monkeys with one of the steel posts.

Missy has also escaped from Snipe and grabbed the thing nearest to her – the bell jar. She lifts it over her head and lets out a war cry so full of rage that even the howler monkeys cover their ears. With a strength no one could have guessed she possessed, she hurls it towards them. Pickingill blows the whistle again, and yet more monkeys swarm down.

Belle and I exchange looks. We have to get that whistle and I realise that there's only one way to do it.

"Up!" I shout, pointing out a rope a few feet to the left of Belle. She nods and I grab one of the curtain ropes on the opposite side to her and start heaving myself up. Belle shins up her rope, faster than any monkey. But I'm only ten feet up when there's a painful twist in my arm; the muscles that once took me up effortlessly have shrunk and weakened and the rope starts slipping between my crossed thighs. Doubt washes over me as I realise I'm not strong enough. I'm dangling pitifully like a conker on a string; sweat prickling my back, when I suddenly hear two low whistled notes. It's Belle, giving our old signal, the one that says, *watch me, sister.*

She makes a simple foot-lock with her rope, slow enough so I have time to copy. First she hooks her leg around the rope, then with her other foot she flips the rope over the first foot to make a loop. As I watch, the memories come flooding back to me. I do exactly as she does, like I'm her shadow, and instead of trying to pull myself up, I *push* myself up with my legs, the rope firm between my feet, my own weight holding it in place. The rope is my friend again. I could stand like this for hours; anyone could, that's the beauty of it. Safe in the knowledge that I can't fall, I edge up into the dark rigging and we find each other.

There's a sudden frightened whinnying. Eight more monkeys have mobbed Apple and cling to his mane and tail. As Apple tries to buck them off, Keziah flips over his bent neck and lands on her back in the sawdust, the wind knocked out of her. Helplessly marooned, she gasps for breath. Another five monkeys scamper up to pin her down. Meanwhile, four of the large spider monkeys have loped across to Missy, and with two hanging on each arm, they start pulling her towards the trap room steps with Snipe barking at them like a sergeant major. Pickingill whistles another command.

"Belle!" I whisper. "If you swing down and knock him over—"

"Then you'll try and grab the whistle!" Belle says, finishing my thought.

She crawls to the far side of the rigging so she can get in perfect position; if she gets the angle wrong, she'll miss him altogether. Belle locks the rope around her legs, then she curls her knees close and lets herself drop. She swoops towards Pickingill, like a wrecking ball, knocking him face-down on the ground. She continues to sail over the stage up towards me and then beyond, even higher. She lands on the edge of some scaffolding and blows me a kiss. I snatch it and lock my legs around my rope the way she did, then I jump.

As I drop past the spotlights towards the floor I know my timing is perfect; Pickingill is clambering back to his feet, pressing the whistle to his lips. I sail by, snatching it from his clenched teeth and soaring back to the rigging above. I land flawlessly and look down to gloat at Pickingill. Instead I find him staring up at me, his eyes triumphant and hard.

There's a muffled scream and I look across the rigging. A group of spider monkeys are wrapping Belle tightly in the safety net. They slowly nudge her off the side and she dangles there, helplessly suspended from a rope that stretches down, right to where Pickingill is waiting onstage. He smiles up at me as he twangs the taut rope with the tip of his finger. Never once taking his eyes off me, he pulls a penknife from the pocket of his dressing gown.

"Always be prepared," he says as he flicks it open and presses the blade against the rope. One slice and Belle will plummet to the ground.

"No!" I plead.

Pickingill doesn't answer but simply holds out his

hand. I have no choice. I throw the whistle down to him. Taking his time, Pickingill smiles and picks it up and blows it. Immediately a group of monkeys surround me. There's nothing more I can do. He's won.

But just as I think all is lost, I hear a rumbling. The noise seems to be coming from the archway we came through and is getting louder. There's a terrible crash, the sound of ripping cloth and a loud trumpeting. Pickingill spins round just in time to see the two elephants burst out from the arch, smashing into lights and trampling the scenery, snorting with fury and flapping their ears. The stage curtain catches in the littlest one's tusks as she shakes her head, then the other tusk gets caught in the backdrop and she rips that down too. They swing their trunks from side to side, knocking the stage columns over before punching through the drums with their feet.

Over the cacophony I hear a jubilant "Yee-hah!" and realise that Rosa is astride the smaller elephant, legs kicked out like a rodeo rider, whooping her arm in the air as if she's swinging a lasso. She gees up her elephant so that it charges towards Pickingill, who is now frozen to the spot, while Snipe dances around him, barking futilely. The older elephant lifts her trunk and makes a deafening sound. Terrified, the monkeys scamper off into the auditorium. Pickingill blows the whistle desperately, but they don't come back. Instead, they clamber up high, clapping with excitement and peeping out over the balconies to see what will happen next.

"Shoo!" Pickingill shouts in a shrill voice as the elephants advance. "Shoo!" He backs away towards the cat and waves his ivory cane at them. But they have had enough of whips and canes. The older one flicks it out of his hand, catches it and snaps it in two with her trunk. Then they both duck their heads and charge at him. I gasp in wonder.

Two sisters, two unstoppable forces of nature.

I glance at Belle. She's managed to wriggle out of the net and is staring down in amazement too. With nowhere left to run, Pickingill grabs Snipe and dives head first into the cat, slamming the door behind him. For a moment the elephants stop, baffled by his sudden disappearance, sniffing the cat automaton. Their huge ears twitch with excitement and I notice Rosa is leaning across their backs and appears to be whispering to them. The young elephant nuzzles her older sister, and they make rumbling noises as if they're deep in conversation, then they lift their trunks and nudge each other in the side.

Synchronised, they put their heads against the giant

cat's rear and shunt it across the stage until it teeters on the very edge, see-sawing for a few moments before it topples into the auditorium. There's a muffled shriek from Pickingill followed by Snipe's shrill yapping, but immediately the elephants trumpet furiously and all falls quiet again. The elephants delicately step down off the stage and press the crowns of their heads against the cat once more, slowly pushing it, until its front legs are squeezed up hard against the first seats.

For a second I wonder if the cat is going to hold or if Pickingill is going to be crushed inside, but then there's a crunching sound and the twang of springs as the first seat flattens beneath the weight of the cat. Then the seats behind the first crumple, one after the other, as the elephants slowly push onwards towards the farthest wall, forging a path until they reach a huge gilt mirror. A family of spider monkeys are crouched under the first balcony of seats and Rosa, always looking for mischief, tugs each of the monkey's tails like a bell-ringer in a church, sending them squealing off into the rigging. I see her whisper into the elephant's ears again and they duck their heads once more and give the cat one final, almighty shove as if it's a battering ram.

There's a terrible splintering crash and the ugly

sound of seven years bad luck as the cat bulldozes through the mirror, the theatre wall behind it and then out the other side. Bricks spew onto the pier and plaster showers down, speckling the elephants white. The wall holds, but there's now a huge gap, which the elephants step neatly through, forcing the cat ahead of them. Belle and I glide down the ropes and race towards the hole. The monkeys scamper past us, flooding out onto the pier's railings or up onto the roof to watch.

The elephants steadily shunt the cat down the pier. When they get to the end, they stop by a set of binoculars fixed to an iron stand, where tourists can watch whales swimming in the bay. I can still hear Snipe barking from inside and Pickingill telling him to be quiet. The elephants swish their tails and flap their ears happily as they remember being free under a star-littered sky.

"What now?" asks Henry, his eyes twinkling.

"Time to get this show on the road!" Belle smiles.

"Would you like to do the honours?" I grin.

Henry giggles and we all hurry out to the mechanical cat. He turns the handle several times until we hear the click that means it's fully wound. Henry looks at us nervously, one after the other.

"Shall I?"

"Yes!" Missy whispers. She lifts his hand and puts it on the firing lever. The door rattles from inside but someone – I can guess who – has bolted it.

"What's happening?" Pickingill snaps from the interior. "You're not going to do anything dangerous, are you?"

Henry slaps the side of the cat. "Safe as houses," he reminds him, then he slams down the lever.

The cat begins to creak and shake as its chest swells and the steel claws slide out. Its eyelids flutter and two beams of light shine over the tranquil sea. Fireworks shoot out of its ears, spitting across the ocean. Then there's a loud twang from inside, followed by a muffled whirring as the cat's jaws creak open. With a sudden whoosh, Pickingill and Snipe shoot through the cat's mouth like a comet, a spray of flames behind them, sailing away towards the distant horizon.

Henry pulls a florin from his waistcoat pocket and I feed it in the binocular slot. The shutters ping open and I look through the lenses in time to see Pickingill pop up, splashing around and yelling. A second later, Snipe pops up too and immediately clambers on top of Pickingill's head for safety. We each take turns to look and laugh before the binoculars whirr and the lenses snap shut again.

"Should we fish them out?" Keziah asks, wiping tears of laughter from her eyes.

Henry shakes his head. "They'll be all right," he says, nodding out at the ocean. "Look!"

We follow the line of his gaze across the sea to the light of a garbage-boat making its journey back to Scoria, taking a day's rubbish to dump on the mainland. As the boat nears Pickingill, it slows and turns its headlights onto him. The crew throw a rope and haul him and Snipe aboard.

As the garbage-boat slowly chugs out of view, we catch one last sight of Pickingill. He's silhouetted against the full moon, with Snipe by his side, sitting on the very pinnacle of Sanctuary's rubbish, like a beetle on a dunghill.

19

Untangling Memories

We are free, but a long way from home.

Keziah says she and Apple will take us back to the Butterfly Circus, and Henry asked if he and Missy can come too; there's nothing left for them on the Isle of Flora since Pickingill burnt his salon down. It will take days before we're home, so we load Enid's caravan with everything we need: food and blankets for us, water and hay for the animals.

I slip outside, carefully picking my way over the rubble and plaster to go and fetch the elephants who are happily stargazing from the end of the pier. High above them, Rosa is sitting on the arm of a lantern-post, her face tilted to the moon. For a moment I think she might be asleep, but then I realise she's moon-bathing, basking in its light. Her eyes are wide open and she's staring up at the stars. As I get closer I hear her muttering under her breath.

"Eight hundred and ninety-four, eight hundred and ninety-five, eight hundred and ninety-six…"

"Rosa?" She doesn't answer. "What are you doing?"

She stares out at the starlit sea. For a moment I wonder if she didn't hear me, but then she sighs deeply.

"One, two, three, four…"

"Are you counting stars?" I ask as I swing my leg up and settle on the railing just beneath her.

"I *was*…" she answers moodily. "You can help if you want. Do that half." She flings her arm in the direction of the Milky Way and I laugh.

"But there are billions of stars!"

"You'd better get started then," she answers. A chill seeps up from the ocean and creeps around the end of the pier. Rosa shivers.

"Come down," I tell her. She slips silently down the post and settles on the railings next to me. Under the halo of lantern-light, she puts her hand into mine and I hold it gently. She can be so strong, but sometimes she feels as flimsy as tissue paper.

"Are you all right?" I ask, pulling the cloak over her shoulders and giving her a squeeze. With Rosa

 201

on one side, the elephants on the other and my sister safe and sound, I feel so happy. I watch a little fish-boat bob past, lifting and dipping on the ocean waves.

"I'm sure I will be," she answers wearily. She leans her head on my shoulder, stretching out her leg. The hole Snipe made has grown into a long tear, running all the way from her knee to her ankle.

"Oh Rosa!" I gasp. "You should have told me!" I should never have let her be my cloud swing; I was too heavy for her. I force myself to put on a bright voice. "Nothing I can't fix," I tell her, dipping my hand in my pocket to find my sewing kit. A few sequins sparkle in the bottom of the tin, like miniature versions of the wishes I saw dropped in the fountain on our first day in Sanctuary.

I bite a length of black silk, take out my smallest needle, hold it up to the moonlight and squint through, then poke the thread in.

"Will it hurt?" Rosa asks. Her voice sounds like it's coming from miles away, from beyond the edges of the ocean.

"I'll be careful," I reassure her, gently laying her leg in my lap. It's strange, but out here, under the shimmering half-light of the stars, I can hardly tell where she ends and I begin. I pinch the edges of the tear together, then ease the needle in, picking up the teensiest scrap of black, no thicker than an eyelash, and make a stitch. Rosa still winces.

"Does it hurt?" I ask, stopping mid-stitch, the thread taut as a tightrope between the needle and Rosa's ankle. Rosa shakes her head and tilts her leg so it's easier for me and I carry on sewing, curling the edges back on themselves and tabbing them down with a neat slip stitch.

"All done," I say at last, knotting the thread so Rosa can't come unravelled. The stitches are so tiny and neat, even I can't see them.

There's a slight gust of wind, sweeping the last remains of cloud from the sky. The moon shines so brightly the ocean seems frosted over. Under the cloak, light drops flicker as Rosa plays with her Glowbell and I realise she's watching me intently.

"It's funny to think you've always been there, right next to me," I say.

As I look into her huge eyes, they turn the deepest indigo and I catch a scent of pine trees again. In the furthest corner of her eye, I think I glimpse a forest at midnight.

"Do you remember?" she asks, so quietly I'm not sure if she said it or I imagined it.

"Remember what?" I say, shivering.

I quickly look away at the elephants as they touch each other's trunks; as if they're saying *everything is all right now*. There's something about this memory of the forest that scares me. But no fear is as hollow as missing a part of yourself, and all of a sudden I wish I could remember everything, even if I am afraid to.

Rosa immediately places her cool hands on my cheeks and fixes me with her gaze. I should feel awkward because I don't like being stared at, but with her I don't mind and I gaze back, looking right into her eyes. I see some tiny spark that catches the light. Up from darkness, something is coming, like something bright being lifted out of deep, dark water.

For a moment I think I'm dreaming, but I can still hear the waves slapping against the pilings beneath us. As I stare into her eyes, the water flows away, and I see a small fire in a kitchen grate, then a girl hunched over a bowl on the table while tendrils of steam lift around her black hair. I look around the room: shrivelled herbs on the window's ledge, a single pink rose in a pot by the door and a careworn woman wearing a cotton apron, with the same ink-black hair as the girl, sprinkling herbs in the bowl. She tells the girl to breathe deeply. The girl looks up and nods. It's Belle.

More steam spirals up from the bowl and the room fills with mist. As it clears, I see a large ship rocking from side to side in the middle of a terrible storm. On the crowded deck, the same careworn woman is clinging to a thin man with sad eyes. Out of the blue, I realise it's my mum and dad, huddled together in each other's arms. I feel a sharp twist of pain in my chest. They place a child into Belle's arms; a child with flame-coloured hair and skin the colour of candle-wax. Then my mum slips her Glowbell around Belle's neck and kisses her goodbye. I look at Belle's wet face; *she* was crying, not me. Sometimes the strongest memories are untrue.

The wind is picking up. Belle is in a tiny lifeboat, crammed with other children. She holds the child tightly to her. My mum and dad edge back as the deck of the ship fills with water. I wish I could see more, but the sun has nearly set and I have to strain to see what's happening on the darkening sea.

The lifeboat sails away from the sinking ship, and screams and blackness spread over everything like a stain. But now, two figures start moving deep in its dark and I see Belle again, holding my hand. We're soaked to the bone, tearing through a forest at midnight. Belle's Glowbell bounces against her chest, flashing rainbows of colour as we run through the black. There's a howl in the distance. She drags me under the bracken, spreading out her green cloak to hide us and cover the tell-tale light of the Glowbell. My mouth is pressed against the pine needles carpeting the forest floor. All I can hear is Belle's heart knocking in fright and her breath ragged in her throat. All I can smell is pine.

After the long night there's a sound of a donkey braying nearby and I pick up the courage to peep out from under the cloak. A huge sun has risen overhead, then suddenly a pair of crinkly eyes peer into the bracken where Belle and I are hiding. And there stands Alfredo Fratellini, sunlight beating down on his faded blue shirt, a minestrone stain on the pocket. I hear his calm voice and then his strong arms slide beneath me as he lifts me up. He's singing a lullaby that he'll teach us later; the one Rosa remembered but I forgot. Belle won't hold his hand at first, but follows him a pace behind as he walks through the dappled sunlight towards a cart where Mrs Fratellini is waiting, stroking the donkey's ears. She smiles when she hears his step and he calls out, "*Cuore mio*! Look what I find hiding under de sap taps – two babes in de wood!"

Rosa lets go of my face and the memory fades away

like smoke. The youngest elephant raises her trunk to sniff the air as if she can smell the tears I'm holding back.

"Are my mum and dad...?" I can't say it out loud. Not yet.

Rosa shrugs sadly. "If that's what you saw. I don't see the memories I keep, not properly. They just pour into me."

"Like water in a well," I murmur, remembering the first night on the railway wagon when Rosa curled up, so round and black like a well of limitless depth. I could tell her my every last secret and she'd never overflow.

"Happy memories are light – they float like feathers. Sad ones are heavy as stones and sink," Rosa whispers.

"That's why you're heavy?"

"Only to you."

"But why haven't I remembered all this until now?"

"You weren't ready, same as you weren't ready to fly again."

"Does Belle know?" I know she does, even before Rosa answers, so Rosa doesn't bother to. I feel disappointment wash over me.

"It wasn't lying," Rosa says quietly, catching the look in my eyes. "It just wasn't the truth either."

I think back to bedtimes when Belle and I talked about exploring the archipelago; the sights we'd see, the people we'd meet. The way she always said it was time to go to sleep whenever I asked what it'd be like when we found our mum and dad again, and if we'd join a circus or have to leave Gala for ever. She *did* have all the answers; she just couldn't bear to tell me.

"Why didn't I realise?" Again I know the answer before Rosa tells me.

"People see what they expect to see, hear what they want to hear," Rosa says.

So what have I been seeing and hearing?

Belle rolling her eyes at me for burning dinner, annoyed at me when I'm late, a slap in her voice when she tells me off. Someone who didn't want me around. The other Belle, the Belle I forgot while I was feeling sorry for myself, is folding a forget-me-not cover over me and smoothing my hair, telling me to picture a hundred islands to explore and not to worry about people she thinks I can't remember. She's had to be a sister and a mum, with no one left to look after her. My disappointment slides into a guilty sadness.

"Why did you keep those memories anyway?" I ask. I regret it immediately but words aren't bubble-gum you can suck back. The youngest elephant nudges me with her trunk as if to tell me off.

Rosa's eyes tinge greyish blue, the colour of hurt feelings. "I don't choose which ones to keep," she explains. "When I'm with you, any sad thoughts you have might fall in. I can't help which ones."

The elephant coils her trunk gently across our shoulders and I give her a stroke. Her sister ambles over to get some attention too.

"Even if I could, memories are like threads. Happy ones can get tangled with sad. That's why I have to keep them all, even ones you think you'd rather forget. There could be something hidden in them you might want back one day. Something you might cherish."

"But they're dead and I never even said goodbye!" I cry. "I can't see how that can *ever* be something to cherish."

"Belle was saved and she saved you," Rosa says softly. "That's what you have to cherish – each other."

I know I do, but tears slip down my face anyway as I think of the broken fragments of my dream. "I thought we'd be together. I thought they were looking for us … but they've been dead all along."

Dead. It's strange but it helps to make that short, blunt word between my teeth and tongue; there's something about it that's as solid as a stone. "Dead," I say, louder this time. But it still isn't loud enough. I climb up onto the top railing and holding the lantern-post for support, I yell it at the top of my voice, out over the vast silence where no one can hear the terrible word skimming its surface.

But the ocean isn't empty.

There's a thunderclap on the horizon and a fountain of foam erupts as two humpback whales breach the waves, an arch of silvery spray in their wake as they twirl mid-air and dive back below. A breath later they crest again, much nearer this time, slamming their flukes again and again on the water, drumming ancient beats until the waves smack against the pier. Water droplets spray up into my face.

"Goodbye!" I yell, as the whales burst though the waves for one last leap, so close together their fins could be entwined. Then they're gone. I watch the exact place they vanished for what seems like hours, until the sea has settled back, smooth as molten silver. I feel a gentle tug at my cloak.

"Are we going now?" Rosa asks.

I nod and she helps me down. Somewhere inside the theatre I hear Belle calling my name, and then she appears in the hole the elephants made, silhouetted against the light.

"We need to get going!" she shouts happily, raising her arm to beckon me in. "Can you bring the elephants?"

"Coming!" I shout, wrapping the elephants' halters around my hand, gently tugging their leash to make them follow me in.

"What were you doing out there?" Belle asks curiously as I approach.

"I was just thinking about Mum and Dad," I say quietly. "They're gone, aren't they?"

The breeze picks up and clouds scud over the moon so I can hardly see Belle's face. It's several moments before she speaks.

"I'm sorry I didn't tell you," she whispers in the dark. "There never seemed to be..."

"The right moment," I finish for her. I know how that is. Without another word, she takes one quick step towards me and holds me tight, then tighter, while far away beyond the horizon, we hear the whales start to sing.

20

Hellos and Goodbyes

I reach the top first. Not because I'm quicker than Belle nowadays, but because I love to have a few minutes up here before we start, just rehearsing my tricks in the dark where no one can see me, or watching the rest of the troupe practise in the ring below. The first time I climbed up into the Hemisphere again, I felt like I'd returned after an exile. I'd forgotten the syrupy dark, the feel of the *corde lisse* between my hands, the smell. Up here under the king pole, the air is warm and sticky, spiced with the scents of rosin, candyfloss and oil for the rigging. But mainly it smells of effort, of tears and sweat permeating every rope. The Butterfly Circus sells dreams, and dreams are hard work.

Two pedestals up from me, Rosa is sitting cross-legged, watching the comings and goings of the troupe below with interest. Beneath us, the ring gleams silver, but it feels like a lucky penny now that I've had so many near misses and lived to tell the tale. I stand up on my pedestal and check my ropes. We have a net now and I'll never fall again. That was Mrs Fratellini's idea. She's the ring mistress; what she says goes.

Rosa watches me tighten the ribbons around my legs. Belle and I are in full costume for the first time tonight, for our dress rehearsal. We're wearing identical outfits that we made together: purple with turquoise swirls of sequins and our wings are gold and silver.

"Want to watch me again?" I ask Rosa, reaching for the aerial hoop I warm up on. I've been practising for hours every day, building my muscles so I'm strong enough to catch Belle. After all these years of being the flyer, I'm learning to be the catcher too.

"I'm fine here," she says quietly.

I grip the hoop firmly, lift my knees to my chest, tip back and poke my feet through the hoop. Once I'm clenching the steel tightly with my knees, I take my hands off and lower myself backwards. Now I'm hanging upside down and swinging slowly through the dark.

 213

Below I see Mrs Fratellini talking to Henry, batting her eyelashes. I've noticed how her eyes are far less beady now that she has someone to be doe-eyed for. She spots me and waves cheerily, patting her newly bouffant hair.

"De one thing de Butterfly Circus needs is good hair!" she had squealed on hearing Henry and Missy's trade, so that's their job. They make wigs and fix the troupe's hair before the shows. Another thing I've learned is that a good hair-do and love seem enough to make people happy. I haven't seen Mrs Fratellini sigh or get teary once since we've been back.

I swing one last time, then hop back on the platform, pulling the silks close. I begin to climb, inching up until I reach the pedestal board just under the one where Rosa is sitting, spinning her shadow Glowbell. Because it's not been in the sun for a while, the light drops are fainter than ever, and against the dark it's hard to see where she is at all.

"You're very quiet today," I say, rubbing a little more rosin between my hands. She doesn't answer. "Is everything all right?"

"Just sorting through my thoughts," she says. I look up, trying to catch her meaning. "A lot has happened to me recently."

"Me too! I can't believe I was afraid of heights and now I'm up here again."

"You should never take yourself for granted," Rosa says. "Before we pulled apart, I never really knew you, but now … I think you're going to keep surprising yourself."

Tears well up in my eyes when I think of the night I met Rosa on the bridge. I remember how scared I was – of her, of heights, of life. She didn't just help me find my sister, she helped me find myself.

Rosa swings her legs for a few moments more and I guess she's deep in thought, then she peers down at me.

"This has been the most fun I've ever had. It's been the biggest adventure of my life." Even though there's laughter in her voice, her eyes are deadly serious.

There's a creak of rope from the opposite platform as Belle jumps up onto her pedestal.

"Tansy!" she yells. "Ready?"

"One sec!" I yell back.

"You know it's down to you that I can fly again?" I smile up at Rosa.

"Yes, it is," she says majestically.

I feel a tremor of excitement surge though my veins as I think about the future and all the other adventures waiting out there. It's going to be so much fun. When

Belle's too busy to play I can hang out with Rosa. I can teach her a thousand tricks.

"You've got everything it takes to be a great trapezist. You're flexible, strong…"

"That's true," she says ducking out of sight again.

"You've got perfect timing, you're not afraid of heights!"

Rosa doesn't answer.

"I can show you how to climb quicker, how to make a basic foot-lock."

There's a long silence from the dark patch where Rosa is sitting. When she speaks her voice is very low.

"I can't…"

"It's easy!" I say, hooking my foot under the silks. "You kick your right leg around one piece, then—"

"I can't stay," Rosa suddenly whispers.

"What?" The silk slips away from under my leg with a low *shusssh*. "What do you mean?"

Just then, high up in the tent's cupola I hear a slither of ropes. Whoever tied the roof flaps together didn't do it properly because a thin slice of moonlight slides in.

"Tansy! Come on!" Belle calls as she starts checking over the trapeze.

"Just putting my tape on!" I shout back. "Rosa?"

"I'm tired." She sounds sad and shaky.

"You just need a bit of sun. It's been cloudy today. Sun always makes you feel better. In the morning—"

"I can't wait until then."

She slides down the rope and lands on my pedestal. I catch my breath in surprise and a knot forms in my stomach; her old, sharp edges are feathering into the air, like ink blots on wet paper. Tiny little threads lift in the moon's shimmer, as if she's moulting. I don't understand what's happening.

"I can fix you," I say gently. "I did before."

"First sign of madness, Tansy." I hear Belle laugh.

But as I look Rosa over, the knot tightens. How do I hem a shape that's shifting? What stitch might work? A blanket stitch? I pat my side, checking for the little tin but remember I left it in the wagon.

"Quickly!" I tell her, pulling the rope towards us to climb down. But she doesn't budge. Instead she puts her hand on my cheek, so light I can barely feel it.

"It's time … look." She holds out an arm.

I peer closer. When I first met Rosa, she was a solid, dense black, so deep that looking into her was like looking out at a starless night. Now I can see straight through her to the platform we're standing on. She's translucent, as thin as the gauze of my butterfly wings.

"Time for what? There must be something we can do?" My voice sounds strangled; the panic is rising, churning up from my stomach.

"It's time for us to join up again."

Across the Hemisphere I hear a low humming as Belle tapes her wrists. Rosa glances across. I wonder if she thinks that now I've got my sister back I don't need her any more. That's not true.

"You can't go," I beg her. "You're my best friend."

There's a rushing sound as Belle swings the trapeze over. Rosa catches it for me.

"I'll be with you all the time. Like I used to be," she says cheerfully, except her eyes don't match her voice.

"But I don't want things like they used to be," I whisper.

Rosa takes my hands and places them around the trapeze. A nut of sorrow hardens in my throat; I know the words I want to say but there's no time left to say them.

"Rosa…" I start.

"I'm not going … I'm coming back," she whispers, then she lays her hands gently over mine so we're holding the bar as one. Even though she's standing right behind me, her voice is so faint I can hardly hear her.

"Tansy?"

It's the first time she's spoken my name.

"Can I keep the Glowbell? For when it's dark?"

My throat hurts too much to speak, but I manage a tiny nod. Then we jump together, swooping across the big top, the night air rushing against my face, my hair flying behind me as we swing into the centre of the moonbeams. At the lowest arc of the swing, at the magical point between falling and rising, I feel a soft breath behind me, the damp brush of silk, then nothing.

I land on the opposite platform.

"You took your time!" Belle laughs, pinching my cheek. "Why are your glasses all foggy?"

She hooks them off, wipes them on her wristband and slides them back on my nose. Then she ruffles my hair, grabs her trapeze and swings back to her place on the other side, ready to start our routine. She gives me a cheerful wave and I keep my gaze fixed on her the whole time. Then, when I'm ready, I look down.

My shadow spills out from my feet like it always did, black and silent; an ordinary shadow, a blockage of light.

* * *

Life keeps changing; keeps being the thing you least expect. I was a famous trapezist, next I was scrubbing floors. One day I was a butterfly then I was a bug. I was sure my parents were waiting to be found, instead they were long gone. I was sure my bracelet had been stolen but yesterday I found it behind the stove where it had rolled. Rosa told me to never take myself for granted. I say never take *anything* for granted.

Keziah took Apple back to her beloved gallopers on Jambor but promised to visit next summer, and I've named the two elephants Jelly and Bean after the sweets Rosa stole for me. Spinnet was nice for a whole week and even stopped called me Bug. But then the nagging sneaked back in, though I don't mind so much, now that I can tell Belle all about it. I still do a bit of selling, mending and poop-picking, but in the evenings, with some added sequins, I'm transformed into the stuff of dreams once more as I fly with Belle.

But my favourite time is night-time, when everyone's in bed, when the dogs are chasing dream-rabbits and barking softly in their sleep. If the moon's bright and full, I slip out of our wagon and creep behind the elephants' house that I white-washed to keep the mosquitoes away. I turn the corner and Rosa is always waiting for me, at her blackest and sharpest. I wave and say hello, and she waves back in perfect time, and we have a midnight feast like the old days, eating the liquorice she loves so much, fluffy from my pocket. We might play with a toy I've brought or I'll tell her a story and show her how to arrange her fingers to make wolves and butterflies. Other times we act out scenes with paper, cut to look like circus tents and sinking ships, because I want to remember my story too; all of it, the happy and the sad. The all of it is all I am.

And sometimes, like tonight, I wonder if I'm imagining things. I wonder if Rosa is just an ordinary shadow, and I'm really just here on my own, making shadow-puppets in the moonlight, while the elephants sleep and sway. But if I lean in and look closely, I can see distant droplets of light flickering around Rosa's heart; her Glowbell, still keeping her dark away.

Acknowledgements

I couldn't have written this book without the generosity of my family; my husband, Olly, who read it and loved it first, then showed me ways to make it better with endless patience. Also my lovely children Charlie, Sam and Rosa, who just get on with it all when I need them to.

And then there are these wonderful women:

Manette, it was your *joie de vivre* I was thinking of when the shadow first skipped into my imagination.

Ariella, my brilliant agent; the sparkle in your eyes when you talk about my stories is what books are written for.

Jane and Sarah, my editors, your passion for books and understanding of this one made it so much richer. Sarah, thank you for so skilfully teasing the threads from the tangle I presented you with.

Sophie, for cheering me on and cheering me up

Last but not least, Ali Hopkins, who never liked being called boss, but was the best one ever, who understood the magic of libraries then worked some of her own on ours. Thank you for gently reminding me of things I shouldn't forget when my head's full of a new story. We miss you and your laughter so much.

Francesca Armour-Chelu writes fiction for children and adults, as well as short stories and plays. She grew up by the Suffolk Coast and studied English and Drama at Goldsmiths, University of London, before working in museum education and public libraries. Her debut novel, *Fenn Halflin and the Fearzero* was shortlisted for the Mslexia Children's Novel Competition 2012 and long-listed for the Branford-Boase Award 2017. The sequel, *Fenn Halflin and the Seaborn* was shortlisted for the Mal Peet Award 2017. Francesca lives in Suffolk and works for Suffolk Libraries.